CANCELLED

The Limbo Ladies

MARGARET YORKE

The Limbo Ladies

SEVERN
SH
HOUSE

376535

This edition published in Great Britain 1992 by
SEVERN HOUSE PUBLISHERS LTD of
35 Manor Road, Wallington, Surrey SM6 0BW.
Originally published in 1969 by Hurst & Blackett Ltd.

This title first published in the U.S.A. 1992 by
SEVERN HOUSE PUBLISHERS INC of
475 Fifth Avenue, New York, NY 10017

British Library Cataloguing-in-Publication Data
Yorke, Margaret
  The limbo ladies
  I. Title
  823.914 [F]

  ISBN 0-7278-4311-7

Printed and bound in Great Britain by
Billing and Sons Ltd, Worcester

All the characters, places, and events in
this book are imaginary.

PART ONE

1

When Sarah Marston learned that her Aunt Hilda had left her a cottage and two thousand pounds, she realised that at last she could leave her husband. It was only the economic problem of supporting Jan and Felix that had stopped her from going before, because she was certain that she could not manage this alone. But now, with somewhere to live and a basic fund, everything was changed. She had a choice.

The letter bringing news of the bequest lay on the mat one morning when she went downstairs in her dressing-gown to make some tea. It was nearly eight o'clock. The patch of sky visible from the kitchen window was a clear, pale blue; the square of lawn outside was fringed with clumps of wispy wallflowers and a few daffodils. Sarah lit the gas under the kettle and then opened the back door, where she stood on the step in the clear, spring air while she read the letter. In the distance she was vaguely aware of the purr of the dairy's van as it hummed towards her, then the chink of bottles dumped on steps. From further off, where the main road passed the end of the Crescent, came the sound of heavier traffic as the workers of Felsham went by car or by bus to work. All but Martin, who had once again found it necessary to be absent all night, for a conference in Hull, he had said this time.

7

Sarah, at first unbelieving, read the letter several times. It was quite definite, the facts clearly stated, not hidden in a maze of legal long-windedness. Bless spinster Aunt Hilda, hitherto considered eccentric, once a suffragette, a schoolmistress, and finally a county councillor, now waving posthumously the wand of a fairy godmother. She had died in Tunis of a stroke at the age of seventy-seven, much to the annoyance of Sarah's father, who had flown out to attend to her funeral arrangements muttering that it was typical of his sister to end her life in unusual circumstances, instead of quietly in the local hospital.

Here was a sort of freedom: a cottage, and some money.

Sarah turned back into the house and dealt with the now boiling kettle. She felt resolute, and charged with energy. The first thing to do was to see Mr. Wilberforce, of Wilberforce, Wilberforce and Wilberforce, Aunt Hilda's solicitor, as soon as possible, to discover how quickly the legacy would come into effect, then she could make plans. Overhead, bumps and bangs indicated that Jan and Felix were awake. In the school holidays she grew lax about bedtime, and they slept later in the mornings. Thinking of the children, she began to weaken; without them, she would have accepted defeat long ago, but the belief that they were entitled to two parents sharing one roof had been her creed for years, and when it at last began to falter she always came up against the problem of money.

Baffled and wretched, blaming some fault in herself, she had pretended at first not to know about Martin's affairs. Some were only guessed at, and some were fleeting, but at the end of each one, Martin always turned to her again and she always hoped it was the last. When, as inevitably happened, the familiar signs of the next began, the absences, the unlikely attentions to herself which were sops to his own guilt, she felt fresh despair. It would never end. She knew now that it was his nature and he could not change. It became nearly impossible for her to talk to him: they rarely quarrelled; they merely lived like strangers in the same house.

He never wanted to marry any of his women. As other men needed fast cars to drive, alcohol, or golf, Martin needed sexual variety. She supposed that he used her and the children to protect himself from possession by each new love in turn. He seemed incapable of enduring affection. Well, this time, and before his latest charmer had begun to lose her appeal, he would discover that Sarah's tolerance had a limit after all. The children, who were fond of him in the intervals when he had time to notice them, might grieve at first, but they were luckily still too young to understand all that was involved. Deciding thus, and invigorated by new hope, Sarah realised that her own self-respect had its value. She had passed through succeeding stages of misery, then rage; finally, numbness had set in. There was nothing she could change. Now this was altered.

Sarah met Martin when she was spending a summer in Cornwall working in a hotel and recovering from a broken engagement. Robin Muir, whom she had known all her life, had fallen irretrievably in love with her own friend Caroline Johnson. When she saw them together, Sarah was aware that between them had sprung up some deep feeling that was very different from the steady affection there had always been between Robin and herself. She buckled on her pride, blessed them both, then fled. Remembering this now, nine years later,

9

and thinking of how she had so quickly lost Martin too, Sarah felt bleak. Perhaps she lacked all ability to inspire a lasting love.

Martin had seemed devoted to her at first; he had pursued her with determination, but she still wondered why he had married her. Perhaps he knew his own errant nature and was trying to protect himself from its consequences by acquiring responsibilities. It was an explanation that, with hindsight, made sense; that, and her refusal to be seduced. She had many times since thought that it would have been better if she had acted differently then. But at twenty-two one could still be idealistic, especially if one had grown up uneventfully in a country village, the daughter of the doctor, with little need for secrets. In her case, it was a classic rebound. Robin was the son of her father's partner, and when they became engaged it was only what everyone had always expected. They might have lived together happily enough if Robin had never met Caroline.

Shrieks from upstairs warned her that the children were getting restive and would soon be demanding breakfast. She got up from the table and began to set out cereal bowls and mugs, and wondered for how much longer she must go on living in this house, performing this task, here in this kitchen. It was coming to an end. Soon, another environment would be as familiar to the children and to her as this one was now. She felt quite calm. Having come to a decision, best carry it out without delay.

She would telephone Caroline, who lived twenty miles away, and ask if she could bring Jan and Felix over to stay for a little while.

2

Aunt Hilda's Mr. Wilberforce turned out to be the middle one of the trio, sandwiched between his elder brother and his nephew. He was a squarely-built man in his middle fifties, with a bald head, pale face, and heavy horn-rimmed spectacles. His office was in the main street of Culverton, a market town near the village where Aunt Hilda had lived.

'Your aunt was very anxious for you to have the cottage. Very anxious indeed,' said Mr. Wilberforce when he had explained the simple terms of the will. He folded his hands together and faced Sarah over a large desk piled with mounds of paper secured in place with books, ashtrays and weights. The walls of the gloomy room were lined with shelves of dusty papers and ancient deed boxes that looked as if they were never disturbed. Perhaps they never were: you died, your papers were stored here, and here they stayed till Armageddon.

'How soon can I move in?' asked Sarah.

Mr. Wilberforce looked surprised.

'Move in? Is that what you plan?' He had expected instructions to sell. The cottage was too far from Felsham to make a weekend retreat.

Sarah saw that she must explain.

'I've left my husband,' she said. 'The children and I are staying with friends. I want to move in to the cottage as soon as possible.'

'Oh dear,' said Mr. Wilberforce, regarding her gravely. 'Oh dear me. How very unfortunate. I'm so sorry. But perhaps it isn't final.'

'The break-up, you mean? Oh, it is,' said Sarah firmly. She saw no reason to enlarge.

At least the young woman was not clamouring for him to obtain a divorce for her, Mr. Wilberforce reflected. Such matters were distasteful to him; he preferred probate and conveyancing. When marital disputes could not be avoided by the Wilberforces, the most youthful of them undertook the business.

'You could take possession of the cottage straight away,' Mr. Wilberforce admitted. 'Of course, I don't know what condition it's in. Your aunt was abroad for some time prior to her death, and she may have neglected things a little.' Anything belonging to the deceased Miss Getteridge was likely to need some renovation, Mr. Wilberforce was sure. His mind's eye showed him his late client, in her ancient felt hat and man's tweed coat, with her spindly legs in wrinkled wool stockings and her feet in brown leather sandals. Yet bizarre though she looked, the old lady's mind had always been sharp.

'My niece may need help one day,' Miss Getteridge had said. 'And she may be too proud to ask her father for it. In any case, he's always been a narrow-minded fool, in spite of what he must have seen as a doctor. Sarah was a promising child. She had spirit.' Unspoken was the comment that Sarah had not lived up to this early hope. 'My nephews need no assistance from me. Security is bad for young men starting out in life,' Miss Getteridge declared. 'But Sarah is in a different position. She has young children, and must ask for money from her husband to buy her toothpaste. How can she pursue a career of her own when she has her family to care for?' She shuddered at her niece's fate. 'I didn't take to her husband,' she went on. 'He's got a weak look about him, like so many men.' Her expression left no doubt but that her legal counsellor was included in this stricture. 'You'll arrange it, Mr. Wilberforce? Plainly and simply? I want no complications.'

He had carried out her instructions, and here was the result: this thin young woman whose honey-blonde hair framed her face in a long bob, and who wore a blue tweed suit the same colour as her eyes. She had a rather desperate look; in spite of his prejudices, Mr. Wilberforce had inevitably acquired a considerable understanding of his fellow humans, and he recognised that Sarah bore signs of strain. That strange old lady must have had some subtle insight.

'Did you see a great deal of your aunt?' Mr. Wilberforce enquired, and his manner had softened.

'No, not much.' Sarah remembered, in shame, how she had joined her brothers in mocking Aunt Hilda, condemning her as a mad old maid with cranky ways. 'She was always very good to me when I was young,' she recalled, thinking of the holiday trips to museums, often boring, and to theatres, more fun; and of Aunt Hilda's visits to take her out from school where embarrassment at her unconventional appearance tended to temper Sarah's enjoyment of the outing.

'Have you seen the cottage?'

'Yes, once. Years ago.' Sarah and Martin had called unannounced on the way back from their honeymoon. Aunt Hilda had been busy weaving at the loom she kept in the living-room, and they had clearly been an interruption to her programme; but she had given them tea and rather burnt gingerbread, and Martin had made fun of her afterwards.

'She visited my parents sometimes. I saw her then,' Sarah explained.

'Would you like to see the cottage now?' Mr. Wilberforce glanced at his watch. 'I fear I cannot spare the time to accompany you, but if you have a car you can get there quite quickly. Or there are buses, but infrequently, I fear.'

'I've borrowed a car,' said Sarah. 'And I'd very much like to see the cottage, please.'

'You remember the way? Well, I'll draw you a diagram, in case you've forgotten,' said Mr. Wilberforce, quickly executing a neat little sketch on a piece of rough paper. 'The turning to Shenbury is off the main road, about four miles out of Culverton. Go down to the church and take the lane opposite. The cottage is the third one past the Post Office.'

'I'll find it,' said Sarah.

'You may as well keep the key,' said Mr. Wilberforce, and as she eagerly took it, he smiled, but so stiffly that Sarah was sure his face seldom relaxed in this way.

'I'll let you know when I'm moving,' she said. 'What about the money? Oh, that sounds greedy and awful, but I haven't any, you see. I'll be getting a job, of course, but I'll need something till then.'

'I take it you are not receiving advice about your matrimonial affairs?' asked Mr. Wilberforce, with a return to his normal gravity.

'No. It's only just happened,' said Sarah. 'And I haven't a lawyer, of course.'

'You have Wilberforce, Wilberforce, and Wilberforce at your services now, Mrs. Marston,' said Mr. Wilberforce, facing the inevitable. 'Perhaps you would like us to act for you. Your husband will be obliged to contribute towards the children's maintenance, and to your own, if you have not—er—if you are innocent of any matrimonial offence in the legal sense of the term. Pressure can be brought, if need be.' He allowed the grim possibility. 'But of course, Mr. Marston may elect to make a satisfactory contribution of his own free will,' he added, with uncharacteristic optimism.

'Oh well, perhaps we'd better find out, if you think so,' said Sarah. 'Meanwhile what do I do?'

'As executor of your aunt's will I shall open a banking account to deal with her affairs pending probate,' said Mr. Wilberforce weightily. He opened a drawer of his desk and took out a cheque book.

'One hundred pounds should suffice for the immediate future, wouldn't you say?' he asked, and at Sarah's startled nod, he made out the cheque.

3

It was a three-hour drive from Shenbury to the Muirs' house, and by the time Sarah arrived back in Caroline's red Mini, after her explorations, the children were all in bed. Caroline and Robin had just finished their dinner, but the remains of a casseroled chicken were keeping hot in the oven for the traveller.

Sarah was obviously tired when she came in, but there was an air of purpose about her that had been lacking for a long time.

'Have a drink, Sal,' said Robin. 'You must need one.'

'Mind-reader,' said Sarah. 'My tongue's been hanging out for the last twenty miles.'

Robin poured her a stiff gin and tonic, and as he gave

it to her, Caroline said, 'Well, tell all. We're bursting with curiosity.'

'Let the poor girl have her drink in peace,' Robin protested, settling himself into his favourite chair. He was a well-built man with mild brown eyes and greying hair that had begun to recede from his somewhat lined forehead, giving him a misleadingly learned look. He was an accountant with a large engineering company, and had recently been appointed to the board, much to his satisfaction and Caroline's unconcealed delight. They were sending their sons to Robin's old school, and talked of buying a boat.

'I'm dying to tell you every detail,' Sarah said. She took a large swig of her drink and launched into an account of her interview with Mr. Wilberforce.

'I ended up feeling almost fond of him,' she said. 'He unbent, finally. Anyway, I found the cottage and had a great hunt about. Phew, what a shambles! It's no roses-round-the-door picturesque gem, I'm afraid. It's made of something they call wychert, which evidently crumbles to dust if it gets the damp into it. It's just kind of mud. But it looks quite sound, outside, and the roof's good. It's rather drear grey slate. The inside's pretty grubby, though. Aunt Hilda wasn't the world's best housewife.'

'Will it need a lot done to it?' Robin asked.

'Well, ideally, yes. A new bath, and so on. But we won't be able to afford things like that,' Sarah said. 'Once it's cleaned up, and perhaps with some white paint slapped on, it'll be fine. Maybe we can improve things as time goes on. I think it's all right structurally. Aunt Hilda was too fly an old bird to let it go really to pot.'

'It's furnished?' This was from Caroline.

'Yes. There's too much stuff, if anything. You know how old ladies are, filling their houses with huge dressers and things. It's all a bit Victorian. I suppose Aunt Hilda got it from her old home when my grandmother died. By that time Father and Mother were settled and wouldn't have wanted it. There's a padded chaise-longue affair in green velvet—rather hideous, but it would be better with a new covering. And there's a rocking chair. But most of the sitting-room is taken up with a huge loom. And there's a potter's wheel in the shed. Aunt Hilda seems to have been a great girl for the handicrafts. I suppose I could sell them.'

'Oh yes,' Robin said. 'There must be incipient potters and weavers about, wanting equipment.'

Caroline thought it time to interrupt.

'You'd better have your dinner, Sarah. You must be starving,' she said. 'Stay where you are, and I'll bring it in for you.'

'Oh, bless you, I'm famished,' said Sarah. She felt exhausted now. The conflicting emotions of the past days had fired her with spurious energy, but there was inevitably reaction, and she had slept very little since she had come to her enormous decision. As Caroline left the room, Robin looked across at Sarah's white face and shadowed eyes. He still felt guilty about her, and would never lose his feeling of responsibility.

As if she read his thoughts, Sarah said, 'Don't start shouldering the blame for me being in this mess, Rob. I was a free agent when I got into it. I'm just thankful I've been given a way out, before it was too late, so you be glad, too.'

'Sarah, my dear, I'm only afraid that you may be plunging into this without giving it proper thought,' said Robin, who had spent hours with Caroline discussing this opinion ever since Sarah had sprung her news upon them. 'You'll find life very difficult on your own.'

'I'm on my own most of the time as it is,' Sarah said. 'I never know where Martin is. This isn't a sudden whim. A person can only take so much, and I've been very bitterly humiliated many times. But how could I pack it in before? I'm no career girl. I could never earn enough to keep the kids on my own.'

'Two thousand pounds won't last very long,' Caroline said, coming into the room as Sarah spoke. She carried a tray.

'It'll subsidise us till the children are older. And we'll have a roof over our heads,' said Sarah. 'And it seems Martin will have to give us some money.' She told them what Mr. Wilberforce had said.

'Well, that's something,' said Caroline. 'Eat up, Sarah, while it's hot.' Like Robin, she had been stunned by the momentous step Sarah was taking with such apparent suddenness; perhaps if she had not kept her troubles to herself all these years, Sarah would have been unable to carry on. Neither Robin nor Caroline had particularly liked Martin, but they had seen very little of him: Sarah and the children usually came over on their own, or if the Muirs went to Felsham, there was some plausible excuse given for Martin's non-appearance. It seemed clear that he had contributed very little to the relationship; Sarah must have had some very lonely years.

'What's Shenbury like?' Caroline asked.

'Well, it's a medium-sized village, with some prettied-up cottages, and a big old manor house, and a council estate. The school's modern,' Sarah replied. 'Oh, and the most amazing thing, I nearly forgot. I was poking about in the shed, investigating the potter's wheel, as a matter of fact, and in came a girl, thinking I was burg-

18

lars or local kids up to no good. Who do you think it
was? Paula Fisher, that I was at school with. She lives
in Shenbury. She used to make pots sometimes with
Aunt Hilda. Isn't that a thing?'

It was. It meant Sarah would know at least one other
local individual besides Mr. Wilberforce.

'It's an omen,' Sarah went happily on. 'Paula was
thrilled to bits when she found I'd got the cottage. Of
course, I was a bit vague about plans. I said I'd get in
touch.' She had finished her meal now. 'That was delicious, Caro,' she said. 'Could you bear to let me borrow
the car again tomorrow, or the next day? That is, if we
can stay with you a bit longer? I want to go over and
have a good scrub round. Then we might move in next
week.'

Robin got up and went over to the fireplace, where
he knocked out his pipe methodically on the identical
brick in the hearth that he always used. Sarah watched
him with amused affection. He was getting very pre-
dictable in his ways, almost pedantic. Such orderliness
could be very irritating. She knew that if she had really
been in love with him all those years ago, the friend-
ship that had prospered between the three of them after
the first awkwardness had worn off would never have
been possible, for she would have been unable to bear
seeing Robin and Caroline together.

'Why don't we all go over at the weekend?' Robin
suggested. 'We could set the kids to work in some fashion, I expect. Could we spend Saturday night at the
cottage, Sarah? We could take the camp beds and so
on. With three of us hard at it, and the kids to fetch and
carry, we'd get a lot done.'

'What a marvellous idea! Would you really? Oh,
Robin, that would be wonderful. There are two beds

there, and the chaise-longue thing I told you about.'

'If we leave at seven, we'd be in Shenbury by ten o'clock,' said Caroline, counting on her fingers. 'We could take a thermos of stew, and when we've seen what's needed, Robin can shop in Culverton for paint, or whatever.' She began to plan with her usual clarity. If Sarah meant this, as she seemed to, then let it be well-organised. 'I expect the children will get in the way, but it will make a good introduction to the cottage for Jan and Felix. They won't find it so strange, later.'

'You could leave us there,' said Sarah.

Once uttered, it sounded very final, even bleak.

'I wish it wasn't so far away,' Caroline said. 'Couldn't you sell it and buy something nearer here, where we could help you?'

'It'd be too near Martin,' said Sarah. 'I've got to get right away, so that he can't come popping in, upsetting us.'

'That's a point, certainly,' said Robin, who was amazed that Martin had not already arrived beating on their door, demanding Sarah's return. So far, she had merely told him that she was taking the children away for a few days, and he had accepted this without any demur.

'Well, why not go somewhere near your parents, then?' Caroline said.

'That would never do. Think what an embarrassment I'd be to them,' Sarah said. 'You know how conventional they are. A bust-up marriage is just something that doesn't happen among Getteridges. They'll be horrified enough as it is, when they hear, without me arriving back home on their doorstep. Anyway, I've got a thing about that cottage. Aunt Hilda was happy there

20

and I'm sure we can be, too. It may sound silly, but I think it's meant.'

Caroline looked sceptical.

'I just hope you aren't making a terrible mistake,' she said.

'I did that when I married Martin,' said Sarah. 'Still, I've got Jan and Felix to show for it, and that's something. If we're going to move at the weekend I'd better go back to Felsham and pack up the rest of our belongings. I'll do it while Martin's at the office, and leave him some sort of hackneyed note, I suppose.'

'He'll come after you,' Caroline said. 'Surely he will?'

'Well, if he does, he can go away again,' said Sarah. 'I can turn him out of my own house.'

PART TWO

1

Sarah stood at the gate of the cottage and looked down the road in the direction from which Jan would appear returning from school, after getting off the Culverton bus at the crossroads. She was late. Her daily fellow-passengers included a group of hooligan boys whom Sarah, in her anxiety, considered near-delinquent, and a few older girls who invited horse-play. There was some bullying, and a good deal of verbal taunting. Sarah was aware that Jan dreaded the journey; she knew also that to escort her to and from the bus stop each day would make things worse, for the other children would jeer still more. Jan was different already because she had no father at home; she must learn to cope with her problems.

It was raining. Sarah wore an old mackintosh, rubber boots, and had a scarf tied over her head. She had been in the shed for the past half-hour, sawing up the branch of an apple tree that had broken in the winter gales. If it was not too green to burn, it would give out a lovely fragrance. Felix, who still went to the village school, was in the cottage having tea with his friend Jackie Phipps who lived at the garage near the cross-roads.

Sarah turned back to the house and opened the kitchen door. The two small boys sat one each side of

23

the table eating dripping toast and feeding crumbs to Dick, the spaniel.

'There's no sign of Jan. I'm going up to see if the bus is in,' Sarah told them. 'Stay indoors, both of you, till I get back. And keep Dick in. We don't want him soaked again.'

'O.K., Mum,' agreed Felix. He helped himself to another slice of toast and grinned at her. He was a plump little boy, with curly brown hair and large blue eyes, and a cheerful disposition.

Sarah left them to it. She pulled her coat collar up round her neck and strode off down the road, the familiar fear in the pit of her stomach. Every day she fretted about Jan, from the time she left home in the morning until she was safely back each night. It had been a matter for such triumph when the child had passed into the High School. Now her education was assured; but it had led to new worries, in the same way that Sarah had shed one set of problems when she left Felsham, only to acquire a new load here in Shenbury.

They had been living at Spring Cottage for three years now, and a big hole had already been made in Aunt Hilda's two thousand pounds, which on Mr. Wilberforce's advice had been put into a building society. It had to be dipped into for school uniforms, a new boiler and a week at the coast after the children had measles and Jan developed pneumonia; and it had to be used to reinforce what came from Martin. Sometimes cheques arrived from Sarah's father, and Caroline handed on outgrown clothes from her children, and some of her own that she had tired of to Sarah, who longed to have an orgy of shopping and buy herself a dress that no one else had ever worn.

Martin had reacted to her departure with great bitterness. He declared that he would divorce her for desertion, and refused to pay her or the children a penny more than the minimum ordered by the court, even though he was earning a considerable salary by this time. Sarah discovered that the residents of Felsham, some of whom she had thought were her friends and whose children had gone to school with Jan and Felix, all condemned her out of hand for leaving Martin. Even those who had known about his philandering ways and felt sorry for Sarah before now nodded sagely, and said she must have asked for it.

Mr. Wilberforce told her that Martin would not be able to bring a divorce suit against her on the grounds of desertion until they had been apart for three years. In the meanwhile, to guard the children's interests, and her own, he advised her to file a petition against Martin. If all that she said was true, it should not be too hard to catch him out. He turned Sarah over to the third Mr. Wilberforce, his nephew, who soon had a sleuth at work and Martin tracked down in circumstances adequately compromising.

Martin never forgave Sarah. It was one thing, in his view, if he pursued other women, but quite another for his wife to prefer life in the depths of the country alone with two children in a primitive hovel, for so he remembered Spring Cottage, to life with him on his terms in a modern house in a prospering suburb. When she took the initiative, his incomprehension turned to rage. He frequently neglected to pay the maintenance ordered; increasingly Wilberforce, Wilberforce and Wilberforce were obliged to press him. He made a great fuss of the children whenever they went to see him, and Sarah had trouble after each of these times, getting them back to normal again. Quite soon after the divorce he married again, a young woman with expensive tastes and bogus blonde hair. They continued to live in the Felsham house, which had been re-furnished and re-decorated from top to toe, according to Jan, who was much impressed by its luxurious new fitments.

Sarah reached the crossroads and looked along the Culverton road. There was no sign of the bus. It was almost dark, and the February rain was turning into sleet. Surely Jan would have telephoned if she had missed the bus? The telephone was one thing which Sarah felt to be not a luxury, but a life-line. Aunt Hilda had scorned it; it would have threatened her independence and unassailability. To Sarah, it was a way of keeping contact with the world outside Spring Cottage.

At the garage, Jackie Phipps' father was pouring oil into the sump of an ancient Morris. Sarah asked him if the bus had passed.

'No, not yet. Reckon it must have broken down, or the driver's stopped at his granny's for tea,' said Mr. Phipps, wiping his hands on a hank of cotton waste.

'Oh, I was afraid Jan was lost,' Sarah said.

'Now then, Mrs. Marston, you worry too much,' said Mr. Phipps, grinning.

'Perhaps there's been an accident?'

'Maybe so, but not a bad one, or I'd have heard, being here,' said Mr. Phipps. 'Bad news travels fast enough.' These women, he thought, for ever fussing. The Culverton bus service was notorious for the elasticity with which it interpreted its timetable.

'Well, I suppose there's no point in hanging about, then,' Sarah said. She stood shifting from one foot to the other, the rain cascading down outside the shelter of the garage. She was reluctant to leave the comforting adult presence of Mr. Phipps, accustomed as she was

26

mainly to the company of children. 'Will you fetch Jackie, or shall I just send him home?'

'You send him, when you've had enough of him,' said Mr. Phipps. He shut the bonnet of the car he was dealing with. 'He'll come to no harm.'

'No, of course he won't,' Sarah agreed. How foolish she was, always imagining imminent disaster. She turned away. There was no point in waiting for Jan, getting colder and damper all the while. If she went home, she could telephone the bus station and find out how long the delay was likely to be, and what had caused it. That, at least, would be a positive action.

She was within sight of the cottage when a dark green Volvo estate car drew up beside her with a swish of tyres, and Jan's excited face appeared at its window.

'Hullo, Mummy! I got a lift,' she cried. 'The bus broke down and Mr. Watson picked me up.'

'Sarah, what on earth are you doing out in this weather? Looking for Jan? Get in, for heaven's sake.' David Watson leaned across Jan and spoke to her through the window.

'I'm soaked. I'll make the car all wet,' Sarah objected, but as David opened the rear door of the car while she was still protesting, she climbed in. He drove the remaining short distance to the gate of Spring Cottage and then stopped.

'There you are, ladies,' he said. 'Right to your door.'

'Thanks ever so much, Mr. Watson,' said Jan, preparing to alight.

'David, thank you for rescuing Jan,' Sarah said. The rain, pouring from her clothes and boots, had made a small swamp on the floor of the car. 'Will you come in? Have some tea.'

'No, I won't, if you'll excuse me, Sarah,' said David. 'I'm expected at home.'

'Of course. Well, thank you again.'

Sarah got out and stood beside Jan at the gate, waving, while he drove off up the lane towards the Manor House, where he lived, at the end of the village.

'Wasn't it luck meeting Mr. Watson? He saw me looking out of the bus window,' Jan crowed, delighted that she had been wafted home in such style ahead of her foes.

'You wouldn't have accepted a lift if it hadn't been Mr. Watson, or someone else you knew, would you?' Sarah asked anxiously. 'You wouldn't have gone with a stranger?'

'No, of course not,' Jan sighed. How Mum kept on. She caught Felix's eye across the table, where the two boys had made a good mess of the loaf and jam left out for them. He winked at her.

Muttering, Sarah departed to take off her wet things, and crossly told Jan to do the same.

2

On Saturday, Paula came to supper. Sarah had made a stew, which she grandly called goulash when Paula produced a bottle of burgundy, in order to up-grade the meal. After the children had gone to bed, the two women finished off the wine, sitting one on either side of the new stove which burned night and day, heating the water, and was cosy to look at when its doors were opened. Sarah was always glad when Saturday came round again; each weekend Paula returned to Shenbury from London, where she was cookery editor on a woman's magazine. Her mother lived in one of the prettied-up cottages in the village. Paula's father had been killed during the war, so that her mother had been alone for a very long time. She was a brisk, cheerful woman who seemed to be perpetually busy; she went to evening classes, helped with village affairs, and was a keen gardener; she played bridge twice a week; and she had been very kind to Sarah.

After Robin and Caroline had driven away on Sarah's first night at the cottage, Paula had appeared. She seemed to understand the situation without explanation, arriving with half a bottle of whisky just as Sarah was on the brink of a panic fit of tears. The children, rather subdued, were in bed, Felix in a camp bed left by the Muirs. They accepted for the present Sarah's sketchy tale of why they were here; persistent questions did not come till later.

'I brought this to christen the cottage,' Paula had said, producing the whisky.

Now, Sarah did not know what she would have done without the Fishers. Almost every Saturday Paula came down for the evening, or sometimes Sarah went to their cottage if she felt able to afford a sitter-in for the children. Occasionally Paula whisked Sarah off to the cinema in Culverton, while Mrs. Fisher stayed with Jan and Felix; and on summer Sundays they often all went off in Paula's car for picnics. It was Paula who, surveying the dismembered loom piled by Robin into the shed, had suggested reassembling it.

'You could sell what you wove. There's a tremendous demand for homespun stuff these days. It wouldn't be difficult to learn to weave a bit better than your aunt did. I often used to watch her and try my hand. She never kept her work even,' said Paula. 'American tourists would snap up what you made.'

The very next weekend she produced a friend who knew about weaving, and several text-books; they threaded up the loom with wool Aunt Hilda had left behind her in a dresser drawer, and Sarah started work. She found an outlet for her wares in Culverton, where there was a shop specialising in modern glass, prints, and costume jewellery. Mrs. Delaney, the owner, bought the lengths of tweed that Sarah wove, and sold them at a handsome profit.

Inspired by this success, Sarah took up potting, too; the wheel, and a large sack of clay, were already there and might as well be used. She and Paula had done some pottery at school, and soon Sarah was able to throw reasonably well-centred pots and vases. Making them marketable meant a problem about painting and firing; she discovered that one of the teachers at the village school had specialised in art, and this young woman became interested. She encouraged Sarah to develop simple designs which she could paint on her pots, and found a local school with a kiln. In return for her help, Sarah lent her the wheel for pottery classes one afternoon a week. Frances Delaney agreed to sell Sarah's pottery as well as her tweed. The amount of money she made in this way was not large, but it helped, and had the merit of being earned in a manner that Martin could not pin down, so that Sarah's alimony was unaffected.

Paula helped to make the shed more weatherproof for these operations. With tongued-and-grooved timber bought at Culverton's Do-it-Yourself shop, they lined the inner walls. A water tap was fitted, and an old porcelain sink found in a junk yard. Sarah bought a paraffin stove so that she could work out there in winter. She wove or made pots while the children were at school, until she felt like screaming; then she whistled up Dick, the spaniel, and went for long, lone walks over the neighbouring fields. As a way of life it worked; she and the children were healthy and well-fed, if shabby; it was a more diverting way of making money than typing in the evenings. Sarah had very quickly realised that while the children were young, going out to a job away from the village each day was not a practical idea. They managed, and they were independent.

Paula poured the last of the wine into their glasses, and Sarah leaned forward to put a log on the fire. It was damp, and spluttered at first, but soon caught and began crackling cheerfully.

'Eric's coming down tomorrow. I'm meeting him off the eleven o'clock train,' Paula said.

'Oh. Is that good?'

Eric was Paula's on-off steady boy-friend. He worked in some obscure department of the B.B.C. and wrote morbid poetry in his spare time. Paula's enthusiasm for him waxed and waned, and Sarah never knew which mood prevailed.

Paula made a face.

'Well, it's meant that Queen Anne's deigned to ask us round for drinks before lunch,' she said. 'She came to pay a state call on Mother—actually it was about bridge, I think, and hearing from our talk that we expected a man in our midst, graciously favoured us. I suppose you're not going?'

'Heavens, no! That'll be the day, when I get asked

to a grown-up do at the Manor,' said Sarah.

'I don't know that I'll bother to go,' said Paula. 'I'll send Eric with Mother, and come down here instead, and throw a few nifty little posset pots.'

'No, you go. You mustn't desert Eric, and you can tell me what gives,' said Sarah. 'I can't go pumping your mother. I expect the house will be full of roses and mimosa. Wow! You may have champagne.'

'Very likely, And poor old David will be looking more like the butler than ever,' said Paula.

Soon after Sarah and the children had arrived in the village, Paula's mother had given a party to introduce Sarah to her friends. It was true that most of the guests at the gathering were women; like all country villages, Shenbury had a high proportion of widows among its population; but there were several couples present too, among them Anne and David Watson from the Manor. A few days later Anne had come to see Sarah at the cottage, expressed approval of the redecorating already done and that still planned, and then invited the children to tea with her own Joanna and Malcolm. Her manner had been regal; she made it clear that Mrs. Fisher's sponsoring of Sarah was what had prompted the invitation. Sarah, then, as now, extremely prickly about her position, disliked the implicit condescension; she soon discovered that Anne adopted a similar attitude to everyone, including her husband, who seemed excessively meek when contrasted with her own forceful personality.

'Well,' Paula continued, 'I suppose we can't altogether blame Anne. You and Mama and I, three women with not a man among us. How could she ask us all at once?'

'I'm never asked, except to some childish function

32

with the kids, and then it's because she knows I'll earn my tea and buns by organising charades or something,' said Sarah. 'Still, I sank my pride long ago. She's been marvellous to Jan and Felix, and given them lots of treats I could never produce.'

'And all on a tide of gin,' sighed Paula.

'You make it sound as if she lives on the stuff.'

'Well, she does. On the revenue from it, if not more directly,' said Paula.

'Good for her. I could do with some of what she's got,' Sarah said. 'She's all right, you know. Once you get used to her queenly ways. She means well.'

'That's the most damning thing you can say about anyone, and well you know it,' said Paula.

'Well, if you were ill, or I was, or your mother, she'd rally round.'

'With grapes and light reading, yes. But would she bring bedpans, if you were that bad? And if she did, she'd make darned sure that everyone knew about her Nightingale act.'

'You're very cynical, Paula. I don't think you're really at all nice,' Sarah observed. 'Not nearly as nice as Anne, for instance.'

'I'd be just as nice as she is if I had her money,' said Paula. 'I bet nothing's ever gone really wrong for her in her whole life.'

'Money can't protect you all the time.'

'No. But it can console you. Anyway, we'd know if anything traumatic had ever happened to Anne.'

'We might not. She can't have lived to thirty-five or however old she is without some troubles,' Sarah said.

'Well, I'm certain they've only been trivial,' Paula insisted. 'But I suppose she doesn't do much active harm, except to poor David. He's been made into mincemeat, right enough.'

'He's probably always been meek and mild,' Sarah said. 'Maybe that's what brought them together.'

'You mean he needed a bossy wife? No, I think Anne crushed him,' Paula said. 'Though he must have known what she was like when he married her.'

'Does one ever?' Sarah asked.

'Well, I know very well that if I married Eric I'd be in for hell,' Paula said. 'Cigarettes stubbed out in the jam, nail trimmings all over the floor, and weirdie friends calling at all hours.'

'Poor Eric. He's not as bad as that, surely?'

'You haven't seen his flat.'

'Well, you aren't going to marry him, are you?'

'On the whole, I don't think so. Only if I get thoroughly plastered next time I'm asked. And even then, I'd still sober up on the brink. One gets tempted to aim at the Partners' Club, sometimes, just because society works that way and one feels one should try it. But I don't think Eric wants a permanent thing, really. He'd be horrified if I took him seriously. He just needs someone to sew his buttons on occasionally, and see he has a bath now and then.'

'Someone else could take him on.' And then Paula would be free to find a less uncouth man. She must meet plenty of them. Sarah loved to hear about the office, and its feuds, and about all Paula's London activities. Since Paula always tried to be entertaining when she recounted her adventures, Sarah had acquired a false impression of the gaiety of her life.

'Perhaps I'd better shop around for a new chap,' Paula said.

'Find one for me, too, while you're about it,' Sarah

said. 'I hardly ever even talk to one these days, except Mr. Phipps or the baker. Perhaps I'd better get a lodger.'

'Where would you put him?'

It was true that there was no room. The sitting-room was totally filled with the chaise-longue, now called the sofa, a sagging but comfortable armchair, and a rocking chair. There was a bookcase along one wall, filled with Aunt Hilda's books and some paperback thrillers that Sarah had bought. A very old television set, handed on by her parents when they bought a new one, stood in a corner. There was no room for extra possessions, and no spare bedroom.

'We'd have to keep him in the shed,' Sarah supposed. But probably the loom and the wheel were less complicated.

3

Frances Delaney, who owned *The Spinning Wheel* in Culverton, and bought Sarah's pottery and tweed, was a widow. She was a few years older than Sarah, and had one son, who was at a minor public school. During the years of their association, she and Sarah had got to know one another well. Frances, who was small and wiry, kept the grey in her hair at bay with an aggressive brown rinse; she wore chic jersey suits, and her spectacles hung round her neck when not in use on a mesh bridle. She was extremely efficient, and her shop, into which she had sunk all that she was left with when her husband died, was a success. She had few intimate friends, but a wide circle of acquaintances, many of them artistic, and some connected with the antique trade, who often seemed to pass through Culverton on their way to sales; they came into *The Spinning Wheel* and drank coffee with Frances, and told her she was wasting her time selling contemporary wares when she could do much better with antiques. But Frances was satisfied with her business; she had discovered by trial and error what sold in the district, and made a good enough living; she was content.

Sarah took in a batch of vases one Wednesday afternoon. It was market day, and Culverton was busy. She carried the pottery, each piece carefully wrapped, packed in a cardboard box that had once held tins of syrup. She went straight from the bus stop to the shop, which was full of customers, women in from the villages around, dressed in thick tweeds and fur-lined boots, and fleecy coats, on this blustery March day. Frances, busy serving, saw Sarah struggle in past a stout lady burdened with shopping bags.

'Have you brought some more pots? Good. If you'd undo them, Sarah, they can go straight out for sale,' Frances said.

Sarah had never seen her wares snapped up with such flattering speed before. The daffodils were out now, and perhaps people liked new vases to put them in. She had evolved a soft green pattern of decoration which would look well with spring flowers. She unpacked her box, and three vases were sold as soon as she put them on the counter. By no stretch of imagination were they genuine works of art: they were merely pleasing; they were not always perfectly regular, and the designs, with their squiggles and stripes on blurry backgrounds, were abstract to say the least.

'I like this, Ethel,' she heard a woman say, holding aloft one of her creations. 'You can see it's hand done.'

So this was it. The lack of symmetry, the imperfections, appealed in an age of mass production. No two of Sarah's efforts were ever perfectly alike.

Frances seemed so busy that Sarah gave up the idea of doing some shopping, and stayed to help her serve, until a lull came when it was time for the country buses to leave.

'I never realised why my pots sold until today,' said Sarah, when the shop was empty, and repeated what she had overheard.

Frances laughed.

'I could have told you,' she replied. 'Your stuff is a trifle unpredictable. It has a unique charm.'

'It chips easily,' said Sarah, who still had trouble with mug and jug handles.

'As long as it doesn't break till they've used it a bit, who cares? We want a good turn-over,' Frances said. She swiftly rearranged a row of Swedish glasses that had been moved by an inspecting customer. 'Thanks for helping, Sarah. I'll get your cheque. What did you bring?'

'A dozen of those middle-sized vases, the ones you sell for six-and-six,' said Sarah.

'Right. Then I owe you forty-eight bob,' said Frances. 'Will you mind the shop while I get it? I'll put the kettle on, too. I expect you'd like a cup of tea, if you haven't got to dash off.'

Sarah glanced at her watch. There was plenty of time before Jan's bus at four-thirty. By travelling on it with her once a week or so, Sarah ensured for her daughter an occasional worry-free trip.

'Lovely,' she said. 'Thanks.'

Frances went away, and Sarah picked up one of her pots. It had a hieroglyph on the base, SM intertwined, her mark. Sometimes an occasional pot said JM or FM, for the children were both promising apprentices, though Felix was still too short to reach easily the pedal that drove the wheel. Forty-eight bob for all that work. Frances had to have her profit, of course; but Sarah's was nearly invisible. Throwing the pots themselves did not take very long, but the painting was slow, and there was the cost of the clay, and the business of getting them over to the kiln to be fired. Jan helped with the painting now; they'd rigged up a turntable on a cake-icing stand, so that the item to be decorated could be revolved against the artist's more or less steady hand.

When Frances returned with her cheque, Sarah, greatly daring, said, 'I suppose you wouldn't put your prices up, Frances, and give me a bit more?'

'Sorry, love. You sell because you're cheap, not because you're an artist. I'm not being rude to you; you know it's true. But your work has taste, or I wouldn't touch it. Ask me again nearer Christmas; we might squeeze a bit more on then.'

Sarah accepted this without protest. She was still surprised that anyone wanted to buy her things at all. She drank her tea and pocketed the cheque. The pottery was more rewarding than the weaving. Results came quicker, for there, under your hands, sprang up a bowl or whatever it was in a matter of minutes; it was satisfying, pressing your thumbs in to make the centre cavity, drawing it up between your fingers and turning out the lip at the top. A bowl was swiftly made, where-as weaving a length of tweed was a long, monoton-ous job. It might pay in the end to sell the loom and buy a small kiln of her own. It would save time, trailing

38

back and forth to get the firing done. But Frances would not want to be saturated with her products; there was a limit to how many she could take. It would mean looking for markets further afield. Faint ambition flickered in Sarah's breast.

Frances interrupted these reflections.

'I'm having a party on Saturday week. It's to celebrate *The Spinning Wheel*'s fifth birthday. Will you come? Drinks and food, about eight.'

'I'd love to. Thank you, Frances. I'll just have to find a sitter, but I'm sure it will be all right.'

'You could leave them. They're old enough.'

'Oh, not yet. Not till the evenings are light, anyway.' But one must eventually. When was it safe to begin? What if the house caught fire, or if they opened the door to a maniac? But on a Saturday night Paula might be the sitter, and might lend her car too.

When she reached the bus stop, Jan was standing on the fringe of a group of chattering children. She was deep in talk with another little girl, and did not see her mother approaching. Sarah watched her with the familiar lurch in her heart of love and anxiety blended. Jan was quiet and sensitive; she found life difficult and seemed cast as a permanent victim; Sarah saw no way to help her toughen up. But it was new and encouraging to see her now conferring with a friend.

'This is Pam,' she was told, when at last she was observed. 'She goes on our bus to Middleton.' Middleton was two miles further on than Shenbury.

Pam was a thin child with a freckled face and long sandy hair. She smiled shyly at Sarah, who thought Jan had found a friend as timid as herself. They sat in a row in the bus, with Sarah at the end, and the two girls chattered together throughout the journey. Sarah did not attempt to do more than seem amiable to Pam; she knew how over-effusiveness made some children retreat. But when she and Jan got off the bus at the Shenbury crossroads, Jan had plenty to say. She told Sarah indignantly that Pam had been kept in at break to re-write her essay on 'How I plan to spend Easter Monday,' because it had been untidy.

'Poor Pam. It's not fair,' Jan declared passionately. 'She never has time to do her homework because her mother's ill and her father's never at home, or if he is, he's drunk.'

Jan said the words in the tone of an adult, and Sarah stared at her, appalled.

'We're much happier than they are,' Jan said.

'Daddy doesn't get drunk,' said Sarah automatically. She wanted the children to retain some respect for their father, and tried to refrain from criticising him.

'No, but he went away. I remember that. And once you were ill, and I cooked lunch,' Jan said. Sarah racked her brain, and remembered an attack of 'flu, and Jan struggling with a bowl of Bovril to her bedside, slopping it on the tray.

'Perhaps Pam could come to tea, sometimes, and do her homework with you,' she suggested. In the past, Jan had always dismissed the idea that any girl should be invited home.

'Yes. She'd get some peace then.' Jan agreed. 'She's got some little brothers and sisters, and they're an awful nuisance.'

'Who looks after them, if her mother's ill?'

'Her granny comes in sometimes,' Jan said.

They reached Spring Cottage. Felix had been told that Sarah would be out when he got back from school, and was instructed to begin his tea. The light was on in the kitchen when Sarah opened the door, and his rubber boots were askew on the floor, but of Felix himself there was no sign, and the house was quiet. Usually he played the radio at full blast the moment he came home.

'Felix, we're back,' Sarah called, taking off her coat.

There was a movement outside the room, and the door opened. A tall, pale young man with rather long brown hair stood revealed.

'Oh, God! Where's Felix?' Sarah, panicking, thrust Jan behind her into shelter.

'Don't be alarmed, Mrs. Marston. Felix is quite all right,' said the young man. 'He had a slight accident.'

There was a faint call from the sitting-room beyond, in Felix's well-known voice.

'What's happened to him?' Thoroughly frightened, Sarah sprang forward to deal with this emergency.

'He had a knock on the head during games this afternoon, so I brought him home,' said the young man. 'When he told me you were out, I decided to stay with him till you came back.'

Sarah was not listening. She burst past her informant and into the sitting-room, where Felix was stretched out on the sofa, looking a little pale and with a small swelling on his forehead, but seemingly with his limbs intact. The young man followed Sarah, and Jan, fascinated, followed the young man.

'Have you called the doctor?' Sarah demanded.

'I was about to do so, but Felix said you would be on the four-thirty bus,' said the stranger. 'He seemed all right, so I left it till you came.'

Sarah pulled herself together. All sorts of horrors had rushed through her mind in the past seconds.

'How do you feel?' she demanded of the patient,

41

whose eyes looked bright and clear.

Felix was enjoying all the fuss. He had a slight head-ache, if he thought about it hard enough, but nothing more. It had been splendid on the football pitch, for he had blacked out for a whole second. He decided to extract the maximum drama from the situation.

'I'm getting better,' he said languidly.

'Faker,' said Jan, from the doorway, undeceived. 'There's nothing wrong with you.'

'You'd better go to bed, and I'll ring up the doctor,' Sarah said. 'Thank you, Mr.—Er—I don't know your name. It was good of you to bring Felix home.'

'Dennis Baker,' said the young man, blushing. 'Not at all.'

4

Felix improved immediately he was put to bed, and demanded to come down again to watch television, but Sarah would not let him. As soon as Mr. Baker had departed, she rang up the doctor, who promised to come round before evening surgery.

Sarah was never good when the children were ill. She felt powerless while whatever was wrong ran its course; she was frightened when control left her hands. Jan's pneumonia after measles was the last occasion on which Dr. Robertson had come to see them.

He was not like Sarah's father, whose grave manner made you fear you must be sicker than he told you. Dr.

Robertson was plump and jolly, and he made you feel better just by his presence in the house. He made a ceremony of inspecting Felix's bump, and discussed football injuries at great length and in gruesome detail with him. Then he said that he thought there was nothing much wrong, but that a day in bed tomorrow, and no more school till Monday, were the prescription.

Sarah led the doctor downstairs.

'He may have slight concussion. If so, a few days of quiet will make sure there's no harm done,' said Dr. Robertson. 'If you let him get up tomorrow he'll probably go charging about the place and you won't be able to keep him quiet.'

'It was too trivial to have bothered you about, I expect,' said Sarah apologetically.

'Oh no. Much better to make sure, in a case like this,' said the doctor. He looked at her sharply. 'You're not sleeping well, are you?' he asked her.

'No, not very well. How did you know?' Sarah said, and then answered her own question. 'I suppose I look such a hag.'

'No, just tired,' said Dr. Robertson. 'A mild sedative will soon put you right.'

'I hate drugs,' said Sarah, shuddering.

'I'm not proposing to give you anything drastic,' said Dr. Robertson. 'Just something to steady you down for a few weeks. Try it.'

Sarah made a face.

'So long as I won't get the habit,' she said doubtfully.

'You won't, I promise,' said the doctor. He scribbled out a prescription for her. 'Can you collect these?'

'Oh yes.' There was time enough. They could wait till she next went to Culverton.

It was rather pleasant having Felix at home the next

day, docile in bed yet not in a grave enough plight for anxiety. Sarah sat by his bed playing draughts with him. His colour had returned, but he seemed sleepy, so after a time she left him with his beloved radio softly playing, and hoped he might drop off for a while. She felt sleepy herself, and decided not to go out to the shed. The work could wait for today. She curled up in the big armchair by the fire and closed her eyes.

She was wakened over an hour later by a gentle knocking on the front door. When she opened it, bemused from being so deeply asleep in the middle of the day, there stood Dennis Baker on the step. Sarah gaped at him while she tried to remember his name.

'Good afternoon, Mrs. Marston. I came to ask how Felix is,' said Dennis.

'Oh! Mr. Baker!' Memory dredged up the detail just in time, and Sarah opened the door wide in hospitable relief. 'Do come in.'

The front door opened straight into the sitting-room. A heavy baize curtain hung on a rod over it, to keep out the draught, and to tangle with the unwary entrant. Dennis, negotiating this, found himself in the presence of what seemed to him to be a goddess in her ambience. Sarah's honey-coloured hair had grown rather long; she was dressed today in slacks and a thick blue jersey; and her face was flushed with sleep. Dennis had thought her lovely but alarming the day before; now she looked vulnerable.

'I've been asleep, I'm afraid,' she explained.

'I woke you,' he cried.

'No, you didn't. I'd just woken up when you knocked,' Sarah civilly lied. It came to her that she had been very abrupt with this young man the day before, first of all taking him for a brigand, and then being

44

scarcely polite, letting him leave with the barest word of thanks and not even a cup of tea. She set to work to put this right now.

'You'll have some tea,' she said. 'I was so rude yesterday, I do apologise.'

'You'd had a shock,' he excused her. He would forgive her anything.

'Well, yes. And I didn't know who you were, you see. Felix hadn't mentioned you.'

'I quite understand,' said Dennis sadly. He was used to making only a small impression on those he met, and he was new at the school this term; he taught Felix only games thus far; small wonder that this fact had not been reported at home.

Sarah went into the kitchen and laid cups and saucers, biscuits, and a piece of fruit cake on a tray. Dennis hovered about while she did this and put the kettle on.

Soon they were seated companionably by the fire, while he told her all about himself. He had planned to enter the church, but lost his sense of vocation, so he had meanwhile become a schoolmaster while he waited to see if it would return. He had taught for two years in Wolverhampton, and was now in Shenbury learning how rural primary schools worked; a very pleasant change, he said.

When Jan arrived home, Mr. Baker was upstairs with Felix, reading *The Thirty-Nine Steps* aloud. He lingered on so late that Sarah was obliged to invite him to stay to supper.

5

As she parked Paula's car in the market square, near *The Spinning Wheel*, Sarah felt suddenly nervous. For days she had been looking forward eagerly to Frances's party, but now doubts and dreads assailed her. Her dress was pre-divorce, like almost all her clothes; it was black wool, very plain, with a high round neck; she had cut inches off the hem before turning it up to a chic length. She had varnished her nails, and set her hair with more pains than usual, so that her long bob had buoyancy. But she was unused, now, to parties, and felt she would be speechless among what was sure to be a crowd of strangers.

Well, here she was, committed; and Paula and Eric were committed too, to an evening at Spring Cottage. Eric had come down again, for a whole weekend this time. When Sarah left, the children were still up, being indulged by their caretakers who were playing Monopoly with them.

She got out of the car and walked round the corner into the alley that led to the rear of the row of shops, where were the private entrances. It was a clear night, and cold, but the wind that had been blowing hard for days had dropped. Sarah went through the unlocked door at the back of *The Spinning Wheel* and up the stairs to Frances's flat.

The usual party noise came down to meet her : gusts of laughter; the sound of music from a record-player; the babble of voices. At least she was not the first arrival. In fact she must be one of the last, she decided, standing on the threshold and wondering how to get through the mass of bodies and into the living-room. Frances, standing near the door with a bottle of wine in one hand and a cigarette in a long green holder in the other, saw her, and gestured to her to push.

'Sarah!' she called. 'Take your coat into my room and find yourself a glass.'

Sarah ploughed through the throng and went into Frances's bedroom. It always intrigued her, with its unusual colour scheme. The big bed had a purple cover; the carpet was black; the walls were white with a purple flowered motif, and there was one tub chair covered in shocking pink. Startling though it was, it worked; but Sarah would not have liked it for her own; it was not restful. But it was difficult to think of Frances resting; she was always busy with something. Sarah added her shabby coat to the miscellany on the bed, and frowned at herself in the large mirror that formed part of one wall. A tall, pale woman with too much hair stared back at her, with large blue eyes ringed with shadows. Her hair was all wrong; she was getting too old to wear it this way. She caught it at the back of her neck with her hand, and wondered about putting it up.

Her musings were interrupted by the arrival of another guest to shed her coat. Sarah released her hair hastily, and smiled sheepishly at the other woman. There was nothing for it, she must face the party.

She made her way out of the room and into the crush of bodies beyond. A man at once thrust a glass of wine into her hand.

'There, darling. That's what you're looking for,' he said, and disappeared.

Sarah sipped. It was a pleasant, rough red wine;

47

Chianti, perhaps. She sipped again, and looked about. As she had expected, there was not a face she knew in sight. Everyone seemed engrossed in talk. She stood, trying to look like part of the furniture, and wondered how soon she might leave.

A man approached, and spoke to her.

'Hullo,' he said. 'I've seen you in the shop, haven't I? Don't you help Frances?'

'I make pots and she sells them,' said Sarah. She recognised him now; he was one of Frances's frequent visitors. 'My name's Sarah Marston,' she supplied.

'Geoffrey Winter. I'm in antiques.'

Sarah asked him about his business, and they talked for some time. He had a shop in London, but he travelled about picking up likely items within quite a wide radius of his base. Sarah enjoyed hearing him explain about his work. He was a stocky man of about fifty, with a florid face, sharp brown eyes and a small moustache, and he had plenty to say so that Sarah did not have to think of much herself. After a while a couple came up to him with cries of joy at seeing him. He introduced Sarah, but the conversation drifted away from her, and eventually so did the trio.

However, it was all right. She would stay a bit longer. The party was going well and Sarah hoped earnestly that someone else would talk to her soon. Before long, a rallying call from Frances heralded the food; everyone was shepherded into the kitchen, where a huge dish of steaming paella and a bowl of dressed green salad waited beside a pile of plates.

It took some time to get everyone served, for only three or four people could get into the kitchen together. In small groups, the guests gathered with their plates, sitting on what chairs there were, or on the floor.

48

Frances had a team of efficient men circling with the wine, so that no glass was empty for long. Sarah was greatly impressed with the organisation of the affair, but then Frances did everything competently. At last Sarah found herself sitting on the arm of a small sofa while she ate her paella.

A very thin, white-haired woman in a bilious green dress began to talk to her. Sarah realised that she was alone too. Out of deference to her greater years, she offered her the sofa arm to sit on, and after some mild protestations they changed places. Sarah then found she was too tall for them to converse with any ease, so she sat on the floor, curling her long legs up under her out of the way.

'Isn't Frances wonderful? Such a lovely party!' enthused White-Hair, picking at her rice.

Sarah asked where she lived, and they made ritual party conversation of the question and answer variety for some time. White-Hair revealed herself to be a poodle-breeder who lived on the fringe of Culverton. Frances seemed to have some widely assorted friends. Sarah wondered how she had acquired this one, who also took part in amateur dramatics.

'I find it a vital method of self-expression,' she declared, in bell-like tones.

At this, Sarah, who had been tossing down as much wine as came her way, and it seemed to keep coming, snorted with laughter. A man standing near her, whom she had been aware of in a vague way as a dark blur beyond her vision, now caught her eye. He had clearly missed none of this. He came towards them.

'Where's your glass, Clarissa?' he enquired of White-Hair, bending down. 'And yours?' he added to Sarah. She saw that he held a bottle of wine, and she turned round to hunt for her glass, just missing crashing heads with the poodle-breeder. By now Sarah felt stiff from her hard perch on the floor, so she untwined herself and stood up, while the man filled her glass.

'I expect Clarissa has been telling you all about her family of dear little doggies,' he said.

Sarah kept her face straight. Her hand did not waver, holding her glass of wine. Clarissa's seemed rather shaky.

'Michael, you are naughty,' she scolded. 'Doggies, indeed.'

Sarah had never before understood what it meant in novels when people were said to bridle; now she learned, for before her fascinated gaze, Clarissa was busy bridling. She stopped when Michael besought her to introduce him to Sarah. This took some doing, for Clarissa herself did not know Sarah's name, and the matter took a moment or two to accomplish.

'I'm sure you never talk to men who haven't been properly introduced, Mrs. Marston,' said Michael, grinning.

'Of course not,' Sarah said demurely. She suddenly began to enjoy herself in a way she had not known for years. 'Why, what would my mother say?'

'And quite right too, with all these dreadful stories in the paper,' said Clarissa, shuddering. She gave Michael her empty glass. 'Put this down for me, Michael,' she commanded, and then to Sarah, 'Where's your husband? Point him out.'

Sarah's cheeks flamed.

'I'm not married now,' she said, and swallowed a defiant gulp of Chianti.

'Oh dear,' Clarissa said, at a sudden loss. She stared at Sarah's wedding-ring.

'Clarissa, I see Betty Smith over there, trying to attract your attention,' Michael intervened. 'Look, by the fireplace. Do go and talk to her. She's much too plump to get over here to you.'

Bridling again, Clarissa was suddenly gone. Sarah and Michael were left together with the remains of the bottle of wine.

'That was neat, wasn't it?' Michael said complacently.

'You mean you sent her on a bogus errand? No one wanted her?'

'Of course not. Can you imagine it? But she thinks so, so she's happy,' said Michael blithely. 'And that leaves us.' He looked at her. 'Where do you live, Sarah-Marston-who-isn't-married-now, and what do you do?'

She told him. Her embarrassment fled, and so did time. She experienced again the sharp pleasure that had begun when they started to talk. After a while they were interrupted by the arrival of plates of fresh fruit salad laced with kirsch, and then Michael was told by Frances that he must circulate with the wine.

'Don't go away, Sarah. I'll be back,' he said. And he was.

It was nearly midnight when she reached home. Paula and Eric were playing gin rummy, and with them was Dennis Baker. They were all drinking beer and smoking.

'Well, no need to ask if you've enjoyed yourself,' Paula said, laying a card down.

'I'm terribly late. I'm sorry. Are you dying to go to bed?' Sarah asked, and then realised that she could have expressed herself more felicitously. She giggled. Paula gave her a look, and winked. The men appeared not to have noticed her remark.

'It's all right. We're quite happy,' Eric said. 'Paula

51

owes me ninepence. And Dennis brought the liquor.'

'Oh—hallo, Dennis.' Belatedly Sarah acknowledged him. She giggled again. 'I think I'm sloshed,' she said.

'I'm sure you are,' said Paula.

'Nice party, clearly,' observed Eric.

'Marvellous. Chaotic, in a way, but organised,' said Sarah distinctly. 'There was a woman called Clarissa, who breeds poodles.' She felt quite proud of herself for articulating this.

'Oh, and who else?'

'Lots of people. Antique dealers and things,' said Sarah vaguely.

And a man, she thought. I met a man.

But she did not tell them.

PART THREE

1

On Tuesday afternoons, Lois Rogers brought her group of handicraft pupils along to Sarah's shed. They used the wheel, and they made clay models, and they spent a pleasant hour. Two of the girls had shown interest in weaving, and they worked at whatever Sarah had threaded up on the loom. She was usually present too, to help Lois, though she could not get on with her own work while the children were there. She mixed up plenty of clay for them before they arrived, and provided tea or orange squash and biscuits after the session.

The little band of artisans trooped up the path, straight to the shed, where if it was cold the paraffin stove would already be alight. They piled their coats in a heap on a chair, and put on their overalls, then set to work. The wheel was the most popular attraction, and there was always a clamour to use it; a few of the children had made some good models, and they all enjoyed themselves. They lived in the village, and at the end of the lesson they went home, while Lois stayed behind to tidy up and have a cup of tea with Sarah. Felix usually arrived as the other children left; much as he enjoyed slapping the clay about himself, he remained aloof from the school potters, and would have nothing to do with their activities.

Lois had been at Shenbury for two years. She was a good teacher, and Sarah thought that Jan's place at the High School had been won chiefly by Lois's efforts. On the Tuesday after the party, the afternoon passed as usual. Eventually the children said goodbye and trooped off to their homes. Felix appeared, flung down his satchel, and announced that he was going to have tea with Jackie. Both boys spent every minute that they could in the forecourt of the garage; they cleaned the windscreens of cars that called for petrol, and often got sixpence for their pains. but apart from this they loved the oily fumes, the roaring noises, and the general atmosphere.

'Shouldn't you take your satchel? Haven't you any homework?' Sarah asked.

'I'll do it when I come back,' said Felix, and dashed off.

Sarah turned to Lois.

'You see,' she said.

'He'll have to buckle down, or he'll never make the grammar school,' said Lois. 'There's time yet, of course, but he's behind in many ways, and he simply won't concentrate. His arithmetic's terrible.'

'I know.' Sarah sighed. 'How awful it is, all these exams, hounding kids all along the line, almost from babyhood. I do make him do his homework, Lois. But short of going through it with him, line by line, what more can I do? He'd far rather be down at the garage with Jackie than anywhere else.'

'Well, of course he would.' Lois felt that Sarah was nearly as resistant as her son. It was in Felix's interests to work hard now, and pass into the grammar school; surely Sarah would not be content for him to develop into a garage hand when he might be a civil servant, with some prodding?

She said this.

'Well, better a happy mechanic than a miserable town clerk,' Sarah said. 'But perhaps the grammar will go comprehensive before Felix gets there, and our problem will be solved.'

'I shouldn't count on it,' Lois warned.

'No. And you're good to be so concerned,' Sarah said. 'I know you push him as hard as you can. I'll have a talk with him.'

Lois pictured Sarah's talk. She was sure that Felix would promise anything, smile like a cherub, and the whole interview would end with laughter all round. Well, perhaps they were happier thus; but it was a pity, because Felix was capable of a good deal if he would only make the effort.

'What are you doing at Easter? Are you going away?' Like Felix, Sarah often sought to evade awkwardness by a change of subject.

'Yes. Peter and I are going walking in the Lake District,' Lois said.

'Oh, how lovely. I hope the weather will be good,' said Sarah.

Each summer, and most spring holidays, Lois went on a walking tour with Peter. He was the man she planned to marry, but he seemed reluctant to commit himself. He was a schoolteacher too, so it seemed suitable, but he was always busy with scouts and summer camps, and boys with problems. Sarah thought it unfortunate that he did not give Lois half the attention he lavished on his pupils, and considered that Lois would do well to cut her losses and count him out of her life.

'Dennis Baker's been here several times since Felix

55

got that bump,' Sarah said now. 'Nice of him to come and enquire, when he doesn't even teach Felix.'

'He will in the autumn, if he stays,' said Lois. 'Maybe Felix will work harder for him, he may need a man.' Especially, she thought, since there isn't one at home. 'Not that Dennis is particularly stern, but the children like him and he can keep order.'

'He seems a nice young man,' said Sarah. He would be a far better bet for Lois than her Peter. Perhaps they never met outside school. That at least could be arranged. Removed from the atmosphere of chalk and inkwells, they might regard each other differently. She would ask them to a meal.

2

As had been the custom for the past three years, Jan and Felix spent Easter with their father. Preparations for their absence were involved; Jackie Phipps took charge of Dick the spaniel, and was to come up to Spring Cottage every day to feed the rabbits, for while the children were at Felsham, Sarah was to stay with the Muirs.

Martin met them at Felsham station. He bore the children off after the briefest exchange of greetings with Sarah. It would be a good thing when they were old enough to manage the journey alone, Sarah grimly thought; maybe they were now, but Jan was never anxious to go at all, and at least Sarah knew they had arrived safely if she handed them over herself, instead of imagining them meeting some awful fate upon the train. Felix appeared not to care where he was, so long as he was fed and housed; now he showed great interest in Martin's new car, hopping along eagerly at his father's side with never a backward glance.

When they had gone, Sarah turned back into the station again. There was nearly an hour to wait before a train would carry her away. She had brought no book to while away the time, and Felsham station was too small to have either a bookstall or a refreshment room, so she was left with just her thoughts for company. She would not go for a walk, for she did not want to risk meeting any of her former acquaintances, who were now the friends of Martin and his wife.

Martin looked sleek, and really rather middle-aged; perhaps he was settling down at last; his new wife might have tamed him. Sarah wondered whether she could have managed to do the same if she had adopted other tactics; retreating into herself, she had withdrawn further still from him, fearful of scenes. Perhaps a few more rows would have brought him to heel, but she could not endure being reduced to a mass of trembling anger. It was all so long ago now, and she scarcely cared any more; Martin seemed a stranger, and it was hard to believe, meeting him again, that there had ever been so much to link them. At a true level of communication, she supposed, there had never been a great deal. She studied a railway poster lauding the merits of a holiday in Ireland, and marvelled that you could live with a man for years and bear his children, yet remain quite remote from him. She felt suddenly bleak.

It would be good to see Robin and Caroline again. Their house was warm and comfortable. She reflected upon the charms of their spare bedroom, with its off-white carpet, yellow bedspreads and thick, soft towels. Lapped in ease, she could forget her responsibilities for a week, and she had better forget Martin and the past, too.

Robin met her, saying Caroline was too busy cooking dinner to come. He kissed her cheek and took her suitcase.

'How are you, Sarah?' he asked, scrutinising her closely before he started the car. 'You're thin.'

'Well, I never carried much surplus, you know,' she said mildly. 'You've put on weight, though, haven't you, Rob?'

'Yes. I don't take enough exercise,' Robin admitted. 'I keep meaning to take up golf again, but there never seems to be time, what with the pressure of work, and the garden, and then visiting the children at weekends.'

Robin and Caroline's two boys were at a preparatory school in Berkshire; Fiona, aged six, was still at home. Sarah knew that Caroline spent a lot of her time baking cakes to send to the boys, lest they starve, and that frequent Sundays were spent in collecting them from their expensive academy and diverting them with museum visits and hotel meals.

Caroline heard the Rover arrive, and came hurrying out of the house to greet Sarah, followed by the children. The boys were almost as tall as their mother; they wore thick Aran sweaters, and had dark, straight hair that fell into their eyes. Fiona was small and plump, young enough still to be kissed and given a hug. They led the guest into the house, all talking at once, and very soon the close-knit family atmosphere had its usual soothing effect upon Sarah; it was like warming oneself at a fire, being in the midst of a united family:

loners like herself needed to be reminded of its strength.

There were new chair-covers in the sitting-room, and Caroline had just acquired a deep-freeze, Sarah discovered in the first minutes. She sat in one of the freshly upholstered chairs and accepted a strong gin and tonic from her host.

'Whenever I arrive in this house, the first thing you do is ply me with alcohol,' she told Robin.

'You always seem to arrive needing it,' he replied. It must be an ordeal for Sarah, confronting Martin, and he knew that she hated having to surrender the children in this way.

There was something very reasurring about Robin at all times, but particularly in moments of stress; Sarah did not know if it was merely the bulk of his physical presence, or simply the fact of his utter dependability. She relaxed. In large doses, Robin and Caroline could be overwhelmingly cosy, so that a prolonged exposure to them might become stifling, but in small amounts Sarah needed them.

Caroline's kitchen was like something from a magazine illustration; as well as the new deep-freeze there was a dishwasher, a fully automatic washing-machine, gay ceramic tiles on the walls and a super sink fitment complete with waste disposer.

'I'm a mean bitch, I'm just plain jealous,' Sarah decided in bed that night. Caroline needed all these things: she entertained a great deal; anyway, they could afford them. Would not she, Sarah, have them if she could pay for them?

The answer was, yes. But this would never happen, and because of their different circumstances, Sarah felt that the paths of herself and her friends were beginning to diverge. It would not amuse Caroline and Robin to rough it at Shenbury for a weekend now; why should they leave their comforts for a slumming trip? If she had remained with Martin, she too might have an ideal kitchen by this time, as her successor had; the children might have had ponies, skiing holidays, and a definite position in British middle-class existence, instead of their present dubious place with a harassed mother dressed in shabby slacks, who occupied a nebulous position. It was the first time Sarah had ever reflected thus; her pride in her own independence had prevented her before.

She stifled these thoughts in the next days, and had a peaceful time helping Caroline decorate the church for Easter with daffodils and lilies, but refused, herself, to attend the Sunday service. Instead, she stayed at the house with the papers, and pretended to supervise the cooking of the capon for lunch, an unnecessary chore because the oven was pre-set and had a glass door through which all could be observed proceeding effort-lessly without human aid. She played cricket with the children, and helped Robin plant peas and runner beans. Being married to him must be dull, she thought; safe, but unexciting. How odd to think that but for a chance she would have been living here with him now, pillar of the district as was Caroline, secretary to the Women's Institute, Brown Owl to the local pack of Brownies. But of course she would not have been these things; she hated such organised activities, and would have been more likely to quarrel with the vicar, and keep goats in the garden, driving Robin frantic with her unconventional ways. At least she was her true self now, ill-regulated in many ways though she might be, and far from self-sufficient, but forced into no alien role. She would have found it hard indeed to have metamorphosed into the rather homes-and-garden woman that Caroline had become, and who suited Robin so well. In fact, had she been content to live like this, she would have accepted Martin as he was, and gone on ignoring his conduct while she built up her material compensations, instead of striking out alone.

When it was time to return to Shenbury, she was glad.

The children were cross and petulant on the long journey home. Jan felt sick, and even Felix refused to pass the time playing 'I Spy,' which had satisfied him on the outward trip. By the time they had trudged from Culverton station to the bus stop, pausing on the way to buy bread and sausages, then waited for the once-hourly bus, tempers were frayed.

'I do wish we had a car, Mum,' Felix said, dumping his suitcase on the pavement with a thud.

'So do I,' said Sarah shortly.

'Dad's new Jag is fab.'

'Very likely.'

'He'll let me drive it soon.'

'You aren't old enough.' This from Jan.

'He will, so there.'

'Are you going to South Africa, then?'

'South Africa? What are you talking about?' Sarah suddenly began to pay attention to her children's words.

'Daddy's going there,' said Jan.

'For a holiday?' People did.

'To live,' Jan said.

'Are you sure?' Jan was not given to wild invention.

'Mm, yes. He told us. And Faith's going too.' This was the felicitous name of the new Mrs. Marston.

Here was news indeed.

'When?' asked Sarah.

'I don't know.'

This would mean an end to these visits which tore at the children's loyalties and wore Sarah's nerves ragged. Each time, they returned over-tired and over-exploited, surfeited with rich food and late hours, and the victims of emotions which they did not understand. This would cease; it would be like a death, finished, and none of them need ever see Martin again.

It was only much later that Sarah realised Martin might be able to leave behind his monetary responsibilities.

'But he won't do that,' she reassured herself. 'He'll still pay up. The children are his, after all.'

Faith must resent them, though, unless she was a saint. She must deplore the fact that a slice of Martin's income must be set aside for this first family; she might see this as the way out; indeed, it had probably been devised as just that.

She would have to see Mr. Wilberforce about it, soon. It was lucky she had heard about the plan.

When they reached the cottage, there was a pile of chopped firewood stacked neatly in the porch, and a bucket of coal; the milk, ordered in advance, had been protected from the tits by a slate laid on the top of the bottles; and Dennis, the good Samaritan responsible for these thoughtful deeds, had written a note of welcome and thrust it through the letter-box.

3

Anne Watson looked out of the drawing-room window across the lawn to where, on the hard tennis court, her children were quarrelling. Malcolm had declared to be out a ball that Joanna knew was in. Anne debated whether to interfere. She was too far away to be a just arbiter. What a pity the two did not get on better together; other brothers and sisters seemed able to play harmoniously, but not this pair. An only child herself, she knew little of how the rough and tumble of family life operated, and would have been mystified if told about natural outlets for aggression.

'I must ask the Marston children up for the day,' she said aloud. 'Are they back, David?'

David Watson had been reading the Stock Exchange news, his ears tuned out from the shrieks in the garden and the mutterings of his wife, who now irritably repeated her question when he did not answer.

'Yes, they must be. There was a line of washing out when I went past,' he said, and returned to his reading. He had, some years ago, inherited the residue of his father's estate; it was very small, but it was his own. He had invested it and watched it slowly multiply; he dreamed of using it to build a house on a cliff top, somewhere far from Shenbury. If Anne were at a meeting, playing bridge, or visiting her parents, and he was safe from interruption, he drew plans of this house, or others he had imagined in his waking hours. David had intended to be an architect, but when he left the army after the war he had already met Anne. She was pretty, very small, and delicate in appearance. For some reason, out of all the men who paid her court, and there were many, she chose David. He never knew quite how it happened. His own desire to cherish what seemed to him a fragile creature was more understandable; he discovered too late how tough, in fact, she was.

She refused to let him finish his training.

'There's no need for that,' she told him, when he deplored the fact that their wedding must wait until he was qualified. Within days her father had offered him a job in his organisation.

David did not give in without protest. His studies were important; he wanted to build houses. But Anne had always managed to deflect him before when he talked about his aims, and she did it now. Surely he wanted to marry her soon, not in several years' time? Well, then, why not snatch this chance? The thought that he might lose her if he delayed influenced David, and this was certainly an opportunity in a thousand; most men would jump at it. He gave in, as Anne's father had foreseen. If she wanted this quiet, dull man, then she should have him; she had never wanted in vain in the past, and it should not happen now; the man was clearly honest and dependable, and would do as he was told. So, without realising what was happening, David gradually lost his independence.

Not long after they were married, David was sent to Culverton as under-manager of a small factory making plastics; it was a newly-acquired subsidiary of the vast empire ruled by his father-in-law. Now he was in charge of this firm, which had been bought especially to provide him with a lucrative niche outside the parent group. Meanwhile, Anne's father had bought the Manor and subjected it to a costly going-over.

David worked hard at the business, and he worked hard, too, in the Manor garden, helped by the full-time gardener who lived in the lodge. He grew asparagus and peaches, and had laid out a water-garden, putting into its creation as much care as would have gone into the building of a house. A little stream ran like a rill, twisting among small shrubs and cascading over stones in a miniature torrent, and it was much admired when the garden was open for charity twice a year, and at the annual village fête. As well as this, David looked after the children's ponies, and much of the time Anne's poodle too. He did his best to earn his keep.

'I'll telephone Sarah in the morning,' Anne said. How like her to have her laundry hanging up where all who passed might see it. Anne had often observed the flapping line of shabby garments. 'I'm sure she'll be glad to have the children out of the way for a bit. I can't think how she can bear to live like that. It was different for that crazy old woman, her aunt.'

'She's got very little choice,' said David. Sarah's lot suddenly seemed to him enviable; at least she depended only on herself.

There came a fresh scream from the tennis court.

'Go and see if you can sort them out, will you, David?' Anne commanded. 'I expect it's Joanna being bossy.'

It probably was. She was like her mother. David put down the paper and went outside. He stood on the terrace and looked at the angry figures of the children. Joanna was clasping her stomach, which a ball had hit, and Malcolm was capering about brandishing his racket, not the least repentant; it was obvious that the injury had been intended. David walked wearily towards them; Joanna had no doubt asked for all she got, but

65

Malcolm was a boy, and would, it was to be hoped, grow up into a courteous man, one who did not strike a woman.

4

Anne enjoyed dispensing bounty. While she waited for Sarah to answer the telephone, she thought of the pleasure her invitation to Jan and Felix would bring. Thanks to her, the two Marston children had learned to ride and to play tennis; they had roller-skated in the yard; they had been to cinemas. It was true that Sarah had helped with the riding and the tennis, and in the intervals between the Spanish couples who came and went as domestic workers at the Manor she had many times turned to in the kitchen when Anne was entertaining for the children, but the main credit must be Anne's. Jan now threatened to play a better game of tennis than Joanna, which was unfortunate, but Malcolm remained the most accomplished of the children. Felix would never present a challenge; cars were all he ever thought of, and he even emitted revving noises from his throat when galloping on a pony.

Sarah was taking a long time to answer the telephone. At length Anne realised that she must be out of earshot, probably in that shed of hers among her pots. Since she was anxious to get the day arranged, Anne decided to walk down to the cottage and fix it up. Trouble taken with the Marstons was worth while;

Sarah might be an odd, gawky creature with unconventional ways, but her children were well-mannered and singularly free of ruffianly ways which they might easily have collected from their school comrades. Anne could do without Jackie Phipps from the garage as a companion for her children, and naturally Sarah must prefer Malcolm as a friend for Felix; the quartet was of benefit to all.

She stepped out down the lane in the warm spring sunshine. The grass on the verges was bright with young growth; in the gardens, daffodils and wallflowers bloomed. A few bees buzzed above the blossoming aubretia that hung in cushions on the stones of cottage walls. Anne, in her hip-length camel jacket, was a neat figure, and she received greetings, all in respectful tones, as she proceeded on her way, from everyone she met, which included three small grimy children swinging on a gate and bad-tempered old Mrs. Smithers who was walking to the shop.

Edith Fisher, Paula's mother, was in her garden pruning her roses. She waved her secateurs at Anne.

'Good morning.'

Anne paused at the white fence that separated Edith's garden from the lane.

'Hullo, Anne. What a gorgeous day,' said Edith. 'I should have done this job weeks ago. Look, doesn't it seem awful to cut down all these lovely shoots?' She brandished a leafy branch of Super Star above Anne's head.

'David does ours in December,' Anne remarked, reprovingly. 'He says it concentrates the growth.'

'I'm sure he's right, but I'm a fair weather gardener,' Edith said. 'I need the sunshine to bring me out.'

It was a fact that Edith, despite ignoring most of the

67

rules, had flowers blooming constantly throughout the year and a herbaceous border that was the envy of the village.

'How's Paula?' Anne always asked after people's families.

'Oh, very well. She's coming home on Saturday.'

'And that young man of hers?'

'I don't know about Eric,' Edith said.

'He's here so often, is it serious?'

'I really don't know, Anne. How does one tell, these days? I think Paula simply finds him useful,' Edith said. In fact she longed for Paula to marry and produce babies that she might drool over, but as time went on and only Eric was exhibited at home, she began to fear the day would never come. 'Paula likes her independence,' she told Anne. 'She's seen plenty of her friends chained to the sink, or come to grief like Sarah. It's made her wary.'

'Yes, Sarah is a warning,' Anne agreed. 'I'm going to see her now.'

'There's nothing wrong, is there?'

'No, I don't think so. I want to ask the children up for the day, but she isn't answering her phone. Potting, I expect.'

Anne continued on her way, and Edith resolved to watch for her return. If Jan and Felix were with her, Edith would ask Sarah up to lunch. She would like to hear how the Easter visit went off, and Sarah probably would not bother to eat anything if she were alone. She did not have enough adult company, Edith knew; she was alone a great deal herself, and had learned to be content with solitude, but she knew that this could be a dangerous state of mind because it led to a gradual withdrawal from participation; for this reason she had built up her own programme of bridge and other ploys.

Sure enough, before long Anne appeared, with Jan and Felix on either side of her. Felix was chattering away in his usual non-stop manner, his hands in the pockets of his shabby anorak, his lower half dressed in tattered jeans. Jan was walking slowly; she looked sulky and rather pale. Of course, she was at a difficult age and was probably upset by the visit to her father. There was something to be said for widowhood; it was at least a clear-cut state, thought Edith, who had lived happily enough with her husband for the years of their marriage before the war, but sometimes wondered now how things would have worked out afterwards if he had survived.

Sarah was sitting on the grass at the end of the garden when Edith found her, cleaning out a rabbit hutch.

'Anne's just carted the children off, when they were in the midst of spring-cleaning,' Sarah said.

'You should have made them finish, and sent them along later,' Edith said. She looked with dislike at a large, sleek buck which Sarah had in a box at her side, covered insecurely with a loose piece of wire netting. Dick, the dog, was eyeing him too.

'Oh, I couldn't do that. Anne wouldn't have liked it,' Sarah said. 'One must co-operate, you know.'

'You shouldn't let her condescend to you,' said Edith. She poked with her toe at the wire, and the buck's long whiskers twitched.

'I don't. I'm jolly grateful for all the benefits the kids get from her, and she knows it. I don't bow down, I just fall into line,' Sarah said.

This was true. Sarah might be hard up, but she was strong on self-respect and proper pride.

'Well, you come and have lunch with me,' Edith

said. 'I've got—' and she paused, '—rabbit stew.'

Sarah burst into delighted laughter.

'Shall I set up as your supplier, Edith?' she asked. 'I'll start a special breeding line, hidden behind the shed, so that Jan won't know.'

Edith frowned at the buck.

'I suppose you keep them to teach the facts of life, being so modern,' she said reflectively. 'Paula had a pony. And we kept a cat. She learned to love them, I suppose. Nothing else.'

There was a lesson here of some sort, but what was it?

5

Sarah returned from lunch with Edith feeling rather gay, and disinclined to spend the afternoon working. But as the children were occupied she felt obliged to seize the chance of an uninterrupted stint in the shed. There was a collection of jugs waiting to be painted; she had better get on with them. She ambled about for a bit, arranging them on the table and setting out her brushes and paints; then she wandered round the garden, inspecting the broad beans that were sprouting strongly and the cloche-covered lettuces, postponing the moment when she must begin. Eventually she collected the portable radio from the cottage and set to work, to the accompaniment of a music programme judged by the B.B.C. as suitable for listeners of all ages.

She daubed away for a couple of hours, managing to keep her mind more or less on the job in hand, until she had finished the batch of pottery and it was ready for the kiln. Then she tidied up her equipment and put her brushes to soak. There was still some time before the children would be home; when they spent the day at the Manor they rarely returned until supper time. She could get on with the tweed that was threaded on the loom; it had been ordered, and the sooner it was done the sooner she would be paid.

First she must wash, and change out of her paint-spattered overall. Sarah did this, then returned to the shed and perched herself on the stool before the loom. She was weaving a simple design in two shades of blue, with a maroon thread in the warp. For a time she worked away steadily, pulling each row taut after the shuttle had sped across. It was monotonous. How many years of her life would be spent thus? she wondered. If Martin really was going to South Africa, and if he vanished as a source of income, she would have to do much more, and the return on her efforts was so poor for the amount of time involved. She needed more lucrative work. She sighed, and sent the weft hurrying to and fro, banging it back after each line. After a while she stopped working and leaned her head on her hands, resting on the finished yardage. Then she gazed round her little empire, grandly called her studio by Jan. It was a pleasant place, warm enough now on this April day not to need the stove. She had tacked bright pictures cut from magazines to the wooden walls, and with the shelf of painted pottery waiting for the kiln, it was bright enough; a jar of pussy willow which Jan had picked stood on a bench, and an ancient basket chair for the use of visitors occupied one corner. But agreeable as it was out here, unless she worked all round the clock she saw no hope of earning a sizeable income, and it was so solitary. Even with the company of the B.B.C., she grew depressed after hours spent alone. She was always eager to accept any chance of a brief escape, such as Edith's invitation had offered.

Should she sell the loom, and buy an electric kiln? This idea kept recurring. She found the quick results obtained on the wheel much more satisfying than weaving. But Frances had said she could not take much more pottery, so she would have to look for other outlets, and her work was not so wonderful when compared with Italian mugs and the produce of other potters. She began to feel rather scared. What would happen when Aunt Hilda's bequest was all spent? If Martin vanished as a source of revenue, it would be gone before the children were able to support themselves. She turned up the wireless loudly to blot out these dismal reflections, and banged on for a few more inches at her tweed.

'I've never seen a hand-loom working before,' said a voice, making her almost jump from her seat in shock. She had drifted off into a day-dream while she wove, and had sped the children into maturity, with Felix in the R.E.M.E., and Jan at Cambridge. Now, brought abruptly back to the present, she turned round and saw that her visitor was Michael Sherard, whom she had met at Frances Delaney's party.

'I startled you,' he said.

'Yes,' Sarah agreed.

For days after Frances's party she had expected him to telephone; when weeks passed with no communication, she slowly accepted that they would not meet again, yet here he was, and laughing at her obvious confusion. She managed to gather up her scattered wits enough to climb from her stool and switch off the radio. The sudden silence was almost more disconcerting than the earlier din.

'I came to see you,' said Michael. 'You never answer your phone.'

'We've been away for Easter,' Sarah said. So he had rung. She thought of the telephone, ringing and ringing in the empty house; how wasteful.

'Show me how this thing works,' said Michael, indicating the loom. So Sarah sat back again on the stool, and showed him how the pedals lifted the separate strands that made the warp, and wove a few rows under his inspection. Michael insisted on having a try, and then wanted to see the wheel and her pots. She explained her problems, and made a small vase while he watched. Sarah was so used to her own creations that she seldom looked at them objectively; now she suddenly realised that they must seem very naive and simple to a sophisticated observer.

'It's native work,' she said abruptly. 'I'm just a peasant.'

'I find it rather charming,' Michael said, carefully setting down the small bowl on the shelf. 'And Frances has a monopoly on it all, has she? I bet she doesn't pay you much.'

'She has to make her profit,' Sarah said.

'I'm sure she sees to that.'

For some reason Sarah felt unable to discuss with Michael the justice or otherwise of her financial arrangements with Frances.

'I'm grateful to her for buying at all,' she said. 'I'm not a very marvellous potter. Shall we go into the cottage?' She swung her long legs round off the stool.

'I expect you'd like a drink,' she added, wondering if there was any alcohol in the house.

Michael followed her up the path that ran from the shed across the lawn and up to the back door. The patch of garden was neatly weeded; various plants which he could not identify were springing up with strong young shoots; he saw rows of vegetables, and what he thought were strawberries behind a rickety paling.

Sarah opened the kitchen door and led the way inside. There was only one bottle of beer to be found in the cupboard.

'Let's go up to the pub,' Michael suggested.

Sarah glanced at her watch. It was nearly seven o'clock. She had worked throughout the afternoon without stopping even for the mug of tea which usually punctuated her spells of toil. The children would be back at any minute.

'I'd love to, but the children will soon be home for supper,' she said. 'They've been out for the day.'

'Well, why don't I go and get a bottle, while you deal with them?' Michael said. 'Then maybe we could go out later.'

Why not? The children would surely come to no harm if she were merely up at *The Angel*.

'Fine,' said Sarah calmly. 'Please share our supper.'

Michael's car, a rather nice Triumph Vitesse, was parked in the lane. He got into it and vanished in the direction of the pub, while Sarah went into the kitchen. As the children would certainly have had an excellent lunch at the Manor, she had merely intended to give them poached eggs on toast for supper, but this would not do now. She inspected her stores. There were some packet soups and a small tin of ham. She rushed down

74

the garden and plucked a handful of chives and some thyme. They would have a large savoury omelette filled with chopped ham.

Michael returned with a bottle of gin and a bottle of burgundy. He found Sarah in the kitchen with an apron on over her slacks, the sleeves of her bright blue sweater rolled up, and her cheeks flushed, peeling potatoes. He thought she looked quite enchanting, and told her so, first putting the two bottles carefully down on the table. Then he came up to her, caught her fair hair into a knot at the nape of her neck with his left hand, and turned her face gently round so that he could kiss her.

Sarah reacted slowly. At first it was if she were detached from the scene, observing it from outside herself as though suspended from the ceiling. She dropped the knife, and then the potato that she held. Then she put her hands, palms outwards, against his shoulders.

'I've got wet hands. I'll dirty your jacket,' she protested, half laughing, but he simply told her to stop talking.

It was years since any man had kissed Sarah, except lightly on the cheek in greeting, as when she saw Rob. She found that the machinery, though rusty, still worked.

'It's like riding a bicycle. You never forget, I suppose,' she said distractedly, pulling away from him as she heard the sound of the children's voices heralding their approach up the path.

Michael had no idea what she meant. However, Jan and Felix came bursting in at this point and had to be introduced. Sarah felt that her cheeks were on fire, and was sure there would be some devastating comment from her offspring, but they were too full of their own doings to be interested in hers. They were both at their best, faces glowing after a happy day in the open, and they had plenty to say. They had ridden all morning, played tennis and climbed trees all afternoon, fried sausages over a camp fire for tea, and then assisted the blacksmith who had come out to fit new shoes to one of the ponies. And they had chicken for lunch. And Mr. Watson had let Felix help him change a wheel on his car when he arrived home from work. Michael leaned against the kitchen wall drinking gin and listening, while Sarah went on preparing the meal and making appropriate comments as the children's tale unfolded. It was a warm, domestic scene. Michael asked questions about the ponies, their names, and their colour, and if they could jump, and wanted to know who won the tennis. He did not enquire about silly things like how old were Jan and Felix, and did they like school. Jan laid the table without being asked, and they all sat down to a feast of soup, omelette and chips, followed by tinned peaches.

'What a spread,' said Felix, letting Sarah down slightly.

'Well, we've a visitor,' she said, and smiled at Michael, not minding this give-away at all. This was what they needed, someone to square them off, a man in their house.

After supper the children wanted to watch television. Sarah gave permission for one programme only, then she sent them to bed, and for a wonder they obeyed at once, tired after their active day.

'We may go up to *The Angel* for a bit,' Sarah said. 'We won't be long.'

'That's all right, Mum. You go. It'll do you good,' Felix said paternally.

'They're a fine pair,' Michael said, when the two had thumped their way upstairs.

'They liked you, too,' said Sarah.

'Are we going to the pub?' Michael looked at her enquiringly.

'Well, aren't we?' In a way she would much prefer to stay at home, and talk. But it would be rather pleasant to walk into *The Angel* escorted by Michael. Some times, but hardly ever, Sarah went in there on her own, and had a glass of beer.

'Perhaps we'd better,' Michael said. He stood up and held his hand out to her, pulling her to her feet. Then he kissed her again, and it was rather a long time befor they did, in fact, go off to the pub.

PART FOUR

1

Frances locked and bolted the shop door, and reversed the sign from OPEN to CLOSED. She pulled down the blind, switched off the front lights, and then went through to the cell at the rear of the shop where she kept her desk and did her paper work. There were orders to make out, and bills to check, so she settled down, put on her spectacles, and started work. She was still at it an hour later when the doorbell at the back rang.

It was Geoffrey.

'Goodness, you already! Is it so late?' she exclaimed, letting him in.

'Well, there's a welcome,' said Geoffrey Winter ruefully, coming into the tiny hallway. He brought with him a disturbing atmosphere compounded partly of his basic male personality, reinforced by a faint aroma of Harris tweed, tobacco, and after-shave, and finished off with emanations of sheer physical energy. He demonstrated this now by enfolding Frances in a determined embrace. She sighed inwardly, not ready for this effort, but suffered herself to be soundly kissed.

'What's the matter, sweetie? Tired?' He began taking off his overcoat, and with his movements filled up the small space in which they stood. Frances took the coat from him, put it on a hanger, and hung it on a hook behind the door.

'Yes, a bit,' she said.

'Well, let's have a little drink, and you'll soon feel better,' said Geoffrey. He set off ahead of her up the stairs, leaving her to switch off the downstairs lights and follow in his wake. A faint irritation rose in Frances. He always preceded her thus, and it always annoyed her. She had taught her son Clive strictly, 'Ladies First.'

There were a good many other things that she found trying about Geoffrey; he cleaned his fingernails in front of her; he wore gaudy socks; and he enjoyed lavatory humour which she found singularly unfunny. Sometimes she wondered how it was that she had let herself get so deeply involved with him; the facts were that when he took her out to dinner for the fourth time, she had one glass of burgundy too many, so that after they came back to the flat she viewed him through a slightly swimming rosy mist, lapped up his catalogue of her charms, and found herself responding in an uncharacteristically ardent manner to his advances. True enough, it was this *premier pas* that counted. After that, it seemed petty to protest; and now she knew that, quibble though she did, she would miss him if he left her life. She often consulted him about matters connected with the shop; he was good-natured and cheerful, and she knew he was genuinely fond of her.

He led the way into her sitting-room, and put on the light. The electric fire was on, and the room was warm. Geoffrey went to the cupboard where Frances kept bottles and glasses, and poured out two stiff whiskies. He gave her one, and tried another kiss.

'Drink up, my dear. You need it,' he said. 'I suppose you've been working at your damned books, have you?'

'Yes. I'd things to see to,' said Frances. She supposed that the best mistressses took a rest before the arrival of their lovers, so as to be at their most alluring. But such wiles were alien to her nature, and anyway Geoffrey never seemed to need encouragement. She sat down on the sofa and put her feet up.

Geoffrey lowered his bulk into the armchair facing her; it was clearly useless to sit beside her yet. He took out his cigarettes and lit one for each of them.

Frances accepted hers and puffed at it; she rarely admitted to fatigue.

'You should get someone to help you, Francie,' Geoffrey said.

She winced at the mutilation of her name.

'You can run to it now. Then you'd be able to have a bit of time to yourself.'

'Oh, I can manage,' Frances said. 'Today's just been extra busy, that's all.'

'You could expand a bit, if you got a helper,' said Geoffrey, who still thought Frances ought to be in antiques, not stocking all this modern stuff.

The whisky was beginning to revive Frances. She must watch it, and not let Geoffrey load her up with drink. Alcohol made her amorous, and she despised herself then for letting her body overrule her brain. Yielding to Geoffrey while remaining intellectually detached was one thing; exhibiting ardour of her own, perhaps unprompted, was another.

'I'd quite like to branch out into stationery. There isn't a class stockist in Culverton for really good writing paper, and greetings-cards, and so forth; and maybe paper-back books, too. The lease next door expires in the autumn, and I'd thought of looking into it,' she said. 'But if I did that I'd really want a partner, some-

81

one who could put some money in.'

A very junior partner, Geoffrey thought, smiling to himself. Catch Frances letting anyone else run the show.

'What about your blonde friend who makes the crooked pots?' he asked.

'Sarah? Oh, I doubt if she'd want to take on a full-time job. She's very tied up with her kids. And as for putting money in, she hasn't got sixpence to bless herself with.'

'She seems efficient,' Geoffrey said. 'And she's a looker.'

Frances pondered this. She always thought of Sarah as somewhat slapdash, but she was business-like over the pottery and the tweed, and had never failed on an order of any kind. And she'd certainly looked attractive at the party.

'She's dependable,' she allowed. 'And we get on. She wouldn't drive me mad, if we had to be together every day.'

'Why don't you sound her out? No harm done,' said Geoffrey. 'You could break her in gradually. You could come away with me sometimes if you'd a stand-in.'

Frances was not sure if this was such a good idea, though she often longed to escape for a spell. At Whitsun and at Easter she went away, and she closed the shop for a week in the summer, but otherwise she never left the town, and had never been to any of the functions parents were invited to attend at Clive's school. But to go away with Geoffrey was not quite what she craved.

He came to see her whenever he was in the neighbourhood, perhaps once a fortnight; he took her out to dinner, and then he stayed the night with her. Rationed thus, he did not take up too much of her time; in a crude way he was good for her, she supposed; and no one suffered any emotional upset. Frances knew that he had a successful domestic life at home; his wife played an important part in the running of his business, and he had two young daughters whom he adored; he might be a little bored after twenty years of marriage, but he would never want to throw them away for her sake, nor would she want him to; small doses of Geoffrey were enough for her.

'You couldn't risk taking me away with you, Geoffrey,' she said. 'Someone might discover.'

'Not if we were careful,' Geoffrey said. 'Mary has no cause to be suspicious.'

Much was implied by this. What hypocrites men were. Geoffrey, like many another, had his life neatly divided up into compartments, each working satisfactorily, independent of the others. Frances frowned. Geoffrey would ditch her without a pang if she imperilled his family life.

Geoffrey saw the frown. He picked up her glass and refilled it. They'd have a Beaujolais with dinner, or maybe a Medoc. Francie was always better when she'd had a drink.

2

On Paula's desk stood a tray with a casserole on it, steaming and giving out a strong smell of onion and leek. There was also a mud-coloured cake that had cracked at the top while baking. Paula's assistant, in a white overall, was sauntering round the room holding a half-eaten slice of the cake in her hand and munching.

'I thought it sounded rather a leaden mixture,' she said, grimacing. 'Why did we think it worth a test, I wonder?'

'Oh, it came from that woman who sent in the good fruit tart, with cinnamon and all,' said Paula. 'I imagined anything from the same stable was worth a second glance.'

'Hm. A fruit tart is a tart, is a tart,' said Judy. 'I didn't rave over that like you did.'

'Mother adored it.' Paula had taken this trial concoction home one weekend.

'Well, this is grisly,' Judith said, and threw the rest of the piece she was eating into the waste-paper basket.

'Must you? I'll have mice playing in here soon,' Paula protested.

'Try the stew. It's like a good vegetable soup, really,' Judith said. 'I thought I'd feed Bill on it tonight, unless you want it.'

'No thanks,' Paula shuddered. 'Vegetable soup at four o'clock in the afternoon is not my idea of a nice tea. You take it away and welcome.' She lifted the casserole lid and peered inside. 'Does it merit a prize?'

'Well, it's very ordinary, but it's good and stodgy, full of potatoes. It'd blunt the edge of a family's appetite all right, pretty cheaply,' Judy said.

'No prize,' Paula decided. 'It's time we found something a bit more exotic for our mums. Glammed-up bangers, in mustard sauce, say.'

'We did that last year,' Judy said.

'Oh, did we? Well, I'm sick of stews, anyway,' said Paula. 'What are you going to do when you're married

84

and have to provide your own food? You and Bill live on our testings, don't you?'

'Very nearly,' Judy admitted. 'I gay them up a bit, with this and that, when I get them home.'

At intervals Paula's column in *Home Fair* ran contests for readers' recipes. None was printed in the magazine unless it had first been tested by the cookery team, and Judy spent most of her time knocking up little dishes in the *Home Fair* kitchen. Sometimes she was photographed in mid-toil, and as she was very pretty, she lent charm to the page. She had been Paula's assistant for two years, and was perfectly content to remain with *Home Fair* until her wedding in the summer. She was engaged to a young man who worked in advertising, and they had a circle of gay friends who more than atoned for the sober worthiness of *Home Fair*.

Paula had left school early because she rebelled against its discipline. To fill up some time, she had been sent to a domestic science school before doing her secretarial training. She started with *Home Fair* as a junior typist; when a vacancy arose in the cookery team she got the post because of her training. She had risen to be head of the section, and often felt very depressed despite having a by-line of her own.

'Why do I stay here?' she wondered aloud. 'I'm sure I'd be better with *Vogue*, or *The Queen*. All this sheer virtue is enervating.'

Judy laughed. Paula often talked like this, and no wonder after so long spent among articles on How to Decorate your Home with Old Christmas Cards, and How to Save Soap (by boiling up the odd ends). Judith had resolved not to stay on after her marriage, in case she turned folksy in due time. She planned to do part-time cooking demonstrations in the intervals of running up curtains and chair-covers for the new flat, and producing delectable meals such as never got promoted in the pages of *Home Fair* because they were too extravagant.

'I really think I'll leave,' Paula said. 'Take these horrid brews away, Judy, and get ready to test fudge. We'll run a sweet-making competition to cheer ourselves up.'

'O.K.' Judy picked up the tray and wandered towards the door, where she paused and turned round, making up her mind. 'Bill and I are having a party on Friday. Eight o'clock. Will you come? And Eric, of course.'

'Oh, thanks.' It was nice of Judy and Bill. Paula and Eric had been to their parties before. They were noisy and cheerful, and everyone else was well under thirty.

Judy was thinking that Bill would shoot her for including them. He said Eric was queer, and maybe Paula too. Judy liked Paula and got on well with her; she was a tolerant boss and had a nice sense of humour; she deserved better than Eric. As for Bill's darker suspicions, Judy told him austerely that he had a tainted mind.

She departed, and Paula, left alone, sniffed at the aroma of leek that still filled the air. She took a fresh-air aerosol from her desk and sprayed it around, then sighed at the idea of taking Eric to Judy's party. It seemed they were labelled a pair for ever. But at that sort of gathering, even without Eric, she would not find another man; they would all be too young, all looking for dolly types eager for sex, no doubt. How difficult it was. She would have to get rid of Eric soon; all he needed from her was mothering, and he took up too much of her time.

She picked up the new copy of *Home Fair* from her desk and skimmed through its pages. The current serial was about the bored wife of a dairy farmer; she dallied briefly with the handsome vet, who though good at his job was a philanderer. Paula knew that in the last instalment the errant wife would realise, just in time, the solid worth of her husband, and the vet would be snared by his female assistant.

'Pah, tripe,' she said aloud, and flung the magazine down. How could people bring themselves to turn out such trash, so far removed from the truth about life? She got up and paced about the room, then looked out of her window at the road below and the glimpse of the Strand beyond. Buses and cars tore noisily by, and people jostled on the pavements. Life was down there, bustling and real: love, death, birth, misery and vice; and some joy, she supposed. *Home Fair* was so home-spun; it was escapist, of course, and fulfilled in that way a function, but it had not moved with the times. Until the present editor retired it was unlikely to alter, though Paula had heard a rumour that the group own-ing it intended to marry it up with one of their more lively productions and so create a new journal alto-gether. This presumably would force Florrie to retire, and some bright spark from outside would doubtless be brought in to preside. Paula knew that she would never be considered for the post, though she might hope to become assistant editor, perhaps. Anyway, this was all some time in the future, and meanwhile here she was, thirty-five years old and with every day predict-able. Her evenings were spent in her tiny flat, with Eric, or else in his squalid room; very occasionally she went to a concert with a girl-friend, or sometimes to the cinema, alone. She enjoyed these evenings very much more than those with Eric, and was developing a new technique of trying to make them possible more often by showing scant enthusiasm for his plans about how they should spend their time. Listening to him reading his poetry or maundering on about feuds, mostly imagined she was sure, in Broadcasting House, was not stimulating.

She needed something new, something more in tune with modern life than *Home Fair* in its present guise. Perhaps she should look for a position with another periodical, or in hardback publishing, before she was too old to make the break. She picked up the magazine once more and looked at the illustration of the simpering wife and the dark, saturnine vet. Life in the country wasn't like that. Take Sarah: if she were a character in a *Home Fair* serial, a handsome young doctor would have come along and snapped her up by now, or a wise, lonely widower with children to bring up. As it was, Sarah's only swain seemed to be that schoolmaster, Dennis Baker, who was at least eight years her junior and who appeared to call on her most days. He was useful; he cut wood, mended things, dug the garden and gave Felix extra coaching, free. Sarah pooh-poohed the notion that he had a crush on her, merely saying he was lonely, but Paula foresaw a day of reckoning.

Of course, there was this Michael Sherard who'd appeared. More might come of that. Sarah, rather excited, had produced him last weekend. It seemed they'd had dinner together once or twice, and been to the cinema, and he'd taken her to *The Angel* several times. But she seemed to know very little about him. He was a writer, producing scripts for television, and he had written two novels. He had rented a cottage on the edge of Culverton. This was all that Sarah had volunteered about him. Writing was a precarious profession, as Paula well knew. What Sarah and the children needed was security; a rock, in fact, like the farmer in the serial.

Perhaps, instead of going to Judy's party, she'd go down to Shenbury on Friday night. Never mind the flat, which she'd planned to clean on Saturday morning; and she'd cancel the appointment she'd made with the man about the boiler; he'd probably forget to come anyway.

PART FIVE

1

Michael arrived just as the children were going to bed. Jan's hair had been washed, and was hanging in damp little curls round her face. Felix, thoroughly scrubbed, glistened; his cheeks glowed, and his hair stuck up in spikes as he stood in the kitchen drinking some milk, in his too-short woollen dressing-gown, with his pyjama-ed legs and bony ankles visible below. Sarah wore an apron; her sleeves were rolled up and her face was flushed. She was very surprised to see Michael, whose visit was unheralded.

'I came to take you out to dinner,' he said, after greeting the childen, and Dick the spaniel, who welcomed him with the same enthusiasm that he would doubtless have shown indiscriminately to a burglar.

'Mike, I can't come out without fixing a sitter. If you'd telephoned, I might have managed something. It's too late now.'

'Mum, you're not going out, are you?' This from Jan.

'No, love. Or only up to *The Angel*, perhaps, for a few minutes,' Sarah assured her.

'We'd be quite all right,' Felix asserted stoutly. 'You go out, Mum.'

'Well, to *The Angel*, maybe,' Sarah repeated. Everyone present knew that *The Angel* did not do dinners. 'Off you go, now. Say goodnight to Michael.'

The children did as they were told, dawdling off upstairs with Jan casting anxious backward glances at Sarah as she went. Something must have gone wrong at school today; she had been subdued all the evening.

'I'll be up in a minute to tuck you in,' Sarah called after them. 'Mike, have a drink?' She knew there was some gin left from his last visit.

'Yes, please.'

Michael watched her fetch the bottle and two glasses; then, as she was about to pour them each a tot, he came and caught her by the arms.

'There's something about the sight of you in an apron with your hair all over the place that does things to me,' he told her.

'I expect you're really looking for a mother-figure,' Sarah said, laughing.

'Not much,' said Michael, demonstrating. He found Sarah tremendously disturbing in a physical sense; he had never before been attracted by domesticity, but the combination of her languid grace and her capable yet casual way of coping with whatever came along was something new in his experience, and it fascinated him.

Eventually she broke out of his embrace.

'I'll find us something to eat,' she said.

'Well, but I wanted to take you out,' he protested.

'That would have been lovely, but you should know by now that if you want to dally with a mother, you must give her time to get things organised,' Sarah said. 'I can always get a sitter if I have some warning.' And ten bob to spare, she added to herself.

Michael stayed. Sarah produced soup and cold ham, and a lettuce from the garden. While she got it ready,

Michael went off to *The Angel* and came back with a bottle of wine.

They had just finished their soup when there was a knock at the door. They stared at one another in dismay across the table.

'Who is it? Pretend you're out,' Michael whispered.

'I can't. Everyone knows I never am,' she replied. 'It's probably someone collecting for the lifeboats, or some such.'

When she opened the door, Dennis stood revealed upon the step, the setting sun behind him surrounding him with a fiery aureole. He carried a large wooden box.

'Oh, Sarah, I brought the new hutch for Algernon,' he said, holding it before him like an offertory.

'Dennis, how kind. Come in,' said Sarah. 'You've been so quick.' She stood back to let him enter the cottage, and he came in eagerly, hunching his shoulders as he stooped under the lintel. He did not at first notice Michael, seated at the table; he had been so single-minded as he dismounted from his motor-bicycle and unloaded his cargo from its pillion that he had failed to take heed of the Triumph parked a little way down the lane. Michael never left it right outside the gate, where the road curved slightly.

'Michael, this is Dennis Baker,' Sarah said. 'Dennis, Michael Sherard.'

'Oh, I didn't see you. Sorry,' said Dennis, blushing brightly. He surged forward, trying to free his right hand in order to shake Michael's, and knocked over a small table as he went. Michael, with visible reluctance, rose to greet him.

Sarah could cheerfully have brained Dennis for appearing at this moment, though had she been on her own she would have been quite pleased to see him. He had become to her someone she was fond of like a rather overgrown Felix; she knew him to be a diffident and lonely young man. However, here he was, and he must be welcomed; he had clearly spent all the evening toiling at the rabbit hutch, the desirability of which had only been mooted the very day before.

'Have you had supper, Dennis? We're just having ours, as you can see. What about some ham and salad?'

Dennis, she knew, had a hearty appetite and could easily put away a plateful of food even if his landlady had provided him with a substantial meal only a while before. Sure enough, he accepted the suggestion at once, though he looked at Michael with frank curiosity. He sat down, while Sarah laid a place for him and carved some slices from the tinned ham.

A constraint then fell upon the trio.

'You were very quick making the hutch, Dennis,' Sarah said at last, seeing that no one else seemed able to think of anything to say. 'Michael, Dennis is a master at Felix's school. He's a very kind neighbour, and he thought the rabbits were running a risk of cannibalism.'

Michael did not share Sarah's tolerance of her children's pets, though he hid this.

'Well, a hutch for each buck is a good idea,' said Dennis.

'You feel they have territorial ambitions, do you, like man in his primitive state?' Michael asked. He picked up the bread knife and sawed himself a piece from the loaf, without asking if anyone else would like some bread. Sarah feared the onset of one of Michael's 'clever' moods, as she thought of them, and sighed inwardly. She also feared for breakfast, looking at the loaf; she had not catered for two visitors this evening.

'Well, hasn't every male, to some extent?' Dennis asked, with spirit. 'Think of all the beasts. And every man, however humble, wants his patch. Sarah, I'll put Algernon in the hutch for you later,' he added, masterfully.

'Oh, don't bother. I'll do it tomorrow,' Sarah said, indolently.

'You might find Claud has eaten him?' warned Dennis.

'Surely they're too big now for that?' Sarah said, 'They fight a bit, it's true.'

'Well, it's an unnecessary risk,' said Dennis. 'Think of explaining to Jan, if one of them killed the other.'

Jan was devoted to both Algernon and Claud, two very handsome gentlemen.

'She's very sensitive, Jan is,' Dennis told Michael, who had observed with resignation Sarah pouring out a large glass of his wine for this most unwelcome intruder. 'She takes things very much to heart. Are they in bed already, Sarah?' He looked about, as if the children might be hiding in the room.

'Yes. They needed an early night,' said Sarah, who had planned one for herself, too. 'Have some cheese, Dennis.'

'Thanks.' Dennis cut a large slab off the square of yellow cheddar, spread some bread liberally with butter, and began to munch. Michael watched him with distaste.

'Do you live in Shenbury?' he asked.

'No, in Hampton St. Lucy, two miles away,' said Dennis. 'I've got digs there. Very nice they are, too, and cheap.'

95

'Don't they feed you?'

'Well, high tea, you know. I'm always hungry again pretty soon,' said Dennis artlessly. 'Have you got any apples, Sarah?'

'In the kitchen. Help yourself,' said Sarah absently. It was slowly dawning on her that these two men were not exactly overjoyed with one another. Dennis pushed back his chair with a scraping sound on the bare floor between Aunt Hilda's old, worn rugs, and went out to the kitchen. 'Anyone else want one?' he called. 'There are some bananas, too.'

'Michael?'

'No, thank you,' said Michael. He had finished his bread, but if he were starving he would accept no food from the hand of Dennis.'

'I'll have an apple, please,' said Sarah.

Dennis returned with two apples and two plates.

'You seem to know your way around here very well, Baker,' said Michael, smouldering at him.

'Well, it isn't very big, is it?' Dennis asked, reasonably enough. 'And I'm often here, aren't I, Sarah?'

'Yes, you are,' Sarah agreed.

'What about you?' Dennis now asked Michael. 'Where do you come from?'

Though the words were ordinary enough, Dennis's tone was definitely hostile, and Sarah intervened.

'Michael's a writer, and he lives at Culverton,' she said.

At this information Dennis perked up.

'What do you write?' he asked.

'Television scripts, and articles, and novels too,' said Michael in a throwaway manner.

Dennis did not waste time on the scripts.

'Novels, eh? Have I read them? Michael Sherard,

did you say?' He screwed up his forehead, trying to place the name.

'*The Necessary Problem. Down Payment,*' said Michael promptly. 'And another on the way, *Ariadne.*'

'I haven't read them,' Dennis decided. 'What are they about?' He thought they must be thrillers.

'Human conflict,' Michael said austerely.

'You should read them, Dennis,' Sarah recommended. Michael had lent them to her, and she had plodded dutifully through them. She found them obscure, and embarrassingly filled with sexual details when you were someone who was acquainted with the author.

'I'll get them from the library,' Dennis promised. 'Do you project yourself into your books? Are they action novels, or stream-of-consciousness?' he enquired with energy. 'Do you identify with your characters? Are they wish-fulfilment fantasies?'

'Certainly not.' Michael was outraged. He glared at Dennis. 'I have no wish to live at secondhand,' he said.

'Oh, I didn't mean to upset you,' said Dennis airily, delighted at the provocative effect of his words. 'You might be doing it subconsciously, without realising you were creating situations in which you'd like to be.'

Sarah, remembering some of Michael's scenes, gave a snort at this.

'Out of the question,' said Michael. 'The ignorant talk a lot of nonsense about a writer's intentions. My books are purely objective.'

'Let's have coffee,' said Sarah pacifically. 'Dennis, will you really put Algernon in the hutch, while the kettle boils?'

'Of course.'

97

Dennis picked up the hutch and strode off into the darkened garden.

'You won't be able to see,' Sarah called after him, with visions of Algernon and Claud escaping into the night. 'Wait while I find a torch.'

'I'll manage,' Dennis answered.

As he disappeared, Michael caught Sarah round the waist and pulled her hard against him, catching her hair back from her face as he always did when he began to kiss her. Her lips were warm and responsive, but her body remained stiff, and she pulled away from him, protesting.

'Mike, not now! Dennis will see.'

'I don't care. Do him good, then he'll know he's not wanted,' Michael growled, renewing his attack.

'Mike, stop it. He won't stay long. We'll get rid of him,' Sarah promised, thoroughly flustered by now.

'You're lovers,' Michael accused.

At this, Sarah burst into laughter.

'Don't be so silly, Michael. We're not people in one of your books. You know quite well that's ridiculous. Anyway, he's years younger than me.'

'That makes no difference. If anything, it makes it all the more probable,' said Michael sulkily.

'Thanks very much. Do you think I'm reduced to cradle-snatching? Things aren't as bad as that,' Sarah said. She managed to free herself from his dissatisfied embrace and began clearing the table. Michael, fuming, sat down on the sofa while she piled the plates in the kitchen. He remained there, glowering, until she came back.

'Mike, you are funny.' Sarah was still laughing at him. 'You're behaving just like Felix when he can't get his own way.' She stood giggling at him, vastly pleased because he was so clearly jealous, even if it was for such a foolish reason.

Dennis returned before Michael could reply.

'Kettle's boiling,' he announced, beaming in the doorway. 'I'll make the coffee. White and sugar, Michael?'

'Very strong, and very black, and sugarless,' Michael growled, reluctantly accepting this unwelcome ministration.

While they drank their coffee, Sarah talked firmly to Dennis about the new school term, now a week old, and Felix's cricket potential, and what about swimming: still no pool at Shenbury; keeping Michael excluded from the conversation. Finally, when the coffee was finished, she rose to collect the mugs.

'Dennis, it was nice of you to come round tonight. Come to supper on Friday, won't you? About seventhirty? Then you can see how Algernon's settling down,' she said, and before Dennis realised what was happening he was outside the cottage, walking unwillingly down the path towards his motor-cycle.

'Poor Dennis.' Sarah fell back on the sofa after he had gone, still giggling. 'That was most unkind. Look how he'd toiled at the hutch.'

'He can console himself by looking forward to Friday,' Michael said, scooping her up in his arms and laying her across his lap.

'I was going to ask you too, Mike, and Lois Rogers, she's another teacher at the school. But you won't want to come now you've quarrelled with Dennis.' This struck her as a very great shame; how delightful it would have been to have engineered a well-balanced dinner party.

'I don't think I'll come, thank you very much, if that oaf's here,' Michael said. 'Stop talking, Sarah.'

He began to make love to her with far more ardour than he had ever shown before, and she, already excited from the tensions of the past hour, was quickly roused. Rather alarmed at herself, she eventually pushed at him.

'No, Mike. Stop,' she said.

'But why? Let's go upstairs,' he urged her. 'Come on, Sarah.'

'No, we can't. The children might wake up,' said Sarah.

'They won't,' Michael said, his mouth upon her neck. 'We'll stay down here, then, if you'd rather.'

'No!'

What if the children woke, and found them? The effect of Michael's insensitivity was like a cold shock to Sarah. She struggled free, pulling her sweater down. He was a writer and should understand these things without an explanation; where was his imagination?

'Well, you must come to my place, then,' said Michael crossly. 'Fix a damned sitter. Let's make it Saturday, since you're occupied on Friday.'

'So that we can go to bed, you mean,' said Sarah carefully.

'Well, we'll have dinner first,' said Michael. 'Silly goose that you are. I'm crazy for you, Sarah.'

It sounded idiotic, said like that.

'But this isn't what I want at all, can't you see?' she wailed, putting her hands to her head. This was a scene she'd imagined taking place many times, but from quite another angle; she needed love, and all that went with it, and had begun to hope that it would come; she did not want this demanding complication in her life.

'Go away, Michael, please,' she said, more quietly.

He tried again. He put his clever hands upon her, but

she turned away, her body stiff, and he had to let her go.

He left the house without another word.

When the sound of his car had died away she flung herself down in the big armchair, weeping bitterly. She wept for loneliness and loss, but she wept also because when he had suggested Saturday, she had instantly thought, yes, I can go, Paula will stay with the children, and she had wanted to consent.

PART SIX

1

Towards the end of May, Sarah's mother came to Shenbury for a few days. She regarded a periodic inspection of the *ménage* at Spring Cottage as her duty, and arrived about once a year to carry it out. After her first visit, when she had slept in Sarah's bedroom while Sarah camped out in Jan's, Edith Fisher had invited her to sleep at Meadow Cottage for the length of her stay, and this offer had been accepted with relief all round. Mrs. Getteridge and Edith remembered one another from the days when their daughters had been schoolgirls together, though they had been merely acquaintances then.

'I don't like to leave Roger too long,' Phyllis said, as she did each year on the first evening when she returned to Meadow Cottage after some noisy hours in her daughter's home. It was pleasant, after the sound of the children's shrill voices and the restless presence of Sarah hurrying about, to sit tranquilly with Edith in her pretty sitting-room for a short chat before bed. Edith had been working at her tapestry when her guest came in; she laid it down to give her attention to the visitor.

'You've had a happy life, Phyllis, haven't you?' she said.

'Yes. Roger and I have been lucky,' Phyllis admitted. 'And the boys have turned out well.'

'So has Sarah. Surely you're not disappointed with her? She does marvels.'

'They're marvels that she shouldn't have to do,' said Phyllis. 'Martin would have settled down if she'd been patient. Women often have to turn a blind eye.'

'Well, yes. But not time and again. And leaving after nearly ten years is hardly being impatient,' Edith suggested.

'Sarah was always headstrong,' Phyllis said. 'Things would have sorted themselves out.'

'You're a doctor's wife, Phyllis. You must see a lot of this sort of thing, or hear about it. Do you really believe a woman should stick it out, no matter what?' asked Edith. 'I don't think, from what she's said to me, that Sarah had any security at all in her marriage. She never knew where Martin was or when he'd be at home.'

'She got her housekeeping money, and she had a home and children,' Phyllis said.

'But at a price. And covering up in front of the children would have got much more difficult when they were older,' Edith said.

'Other people manage,' said Phyllis. 'Everyone has some sort of difficulty. Roger and I had to struggle for years to get the practice established. We were hard up for a long time.'

'I don't think Sarah ever expected life to be easy,' said Edith. 'She just expected honest treatment. At least she knows where she is now. It's hard, bringing up children on your own, believe me, and I only had one to cope with.'

'Oh, I'm sure she does her best,' Phyllis said. 'Things would have been different if she'd married Robin, of course. He and Caroline have a lovely house and such sweet children. That was a great pity.'

'Well, these things happen.' Edith picked up her sew-
ing again; perhaps she could fill in some of the background while they talked. What was the use of trying
to make Phyllis see things from a more tolerant angle?
Would it really help Sarah if she persevered?

'Jan and Felix look so rough. They're polite, of course,
and seem healthy, but they're quite unlike my other
grandchildren,' Phyllis said.

'Sarah is not as well-off as her brothers, is she?'
Edith said promply.

'Well, Roger can't do any more for her,' said Phyllis,
as if he had been openly criticised. 'He sends her what
he can.'

It was indeed harsh if adult children, who should be
set in life, suddenly needed subsidising by their parents.
Edith knew that from time to time a cheque arrived
from Dr. Getteridge.

'Anyway, why should he? Martin can't expect to
escape from his responsibilities,' Phyllis added.

'How are your other grandchildren?' Edith decided
it was time to change the subject. Sarah's brothers were
both a credit to their parents, and had produced exem-
plary children who passed exams and could be bragged
about. It seemed strange to Edith that Phyllis should
have so little sympathy with her only daughter; Edith
would have expected her to take Sarah's part no matter
what. In her view, Sarah was to be admired; she seldom
gave way openly to depression; in fact, her spirit seemed to increase all the time. Edith had great fellow-feel-
ing for her and her problems. Perhaps the very success
of Phyllis's marriage made her imperceptive about what
went on outside it, as though she were protected by it,
encapsulated, wrapped protectively against the world.

How very dull her life must be, thought Edith, and envied her not at all, slave as she was to the telephone and her duty of guarding Roger from over-importunate patients.

She drew out a strand of rose-coloured wool and threaded her needle, preparing to listen patiently to a recital of the virtues of Phyllis's sons' children.

2

'How's your mother's visit going?' Frances asked.

Sarah had been shopping in Culverton. Her mother was having her hair done at *Madeleine*'s, four doors down from *The Spinning Wheel*, and was later taking both Sarah and Frances out to lunch at *The Bell*. Felix was having his meal at school today.

'Oh, all right, I suppose.' Sarah shifted a glass bowl forward on the shelf. 'This is nice. Swedish, is it?'

'Yes.'

Frances waited. She knew that Sarah had looked forward to her mother's visit with both pleasure and dread; she longed for maternal approbation, yet never seemed to win it. She always expected Jan or Felix, if not she herself, to offend, and her one aim was to get through the day without giving cause for complaint. She looked tired, Frances thought, and pale; she wore her old blue suit, and by the way it hung round her had lost a lot of weight.

'Mother doesn't really approve of our set-up, you

know that,' Sarah said at last. 'She likes people to conform, especially her relations. We're a bit off-beat, by her standards, what with pottery in the parlour, as you might say, and frank speech at all times. She believes in brushing away the nastiness under the carpet and then you can pretend it isn't there.'

'She's jolly lucky if she can ignore it, these days,' Frances said.

'I think she's ashamed of me,' said Sarah sadly. 'It would be different if I were a widow, like you. Then she could be sorry for me. But I've failed at marriage, woman's vital function, something she's done well. I can just feel her disapproving of us all the time—you know, Felix eating with his mouth open, and Jan frightened of school, and me so shabby.'

'You're probably a bit over-prickly, Sarah,' Frances said. 'We limbo ladies often are hyper-sensitive.'

'Limbo ladies? What do you mean?'

'Oh, the state in which we live. Manless women of our age exist in a social limbo, don't you agree? It's different when you're younger. But after about, say, thirty-two or so, the pattern is, tidy pairs, and anyone who isn't neatly partnered off is out of the club. I found, after Tom died, once I'd had time to get over it and so on, that people who'd been very kind at first gradually dropped me. They just didn't want to know. Maybe the wives thought I'd chase their husbands, I don't know. A surplus woman is an embarrassment in a community, a surplus man a boon.'

Sarah was staring at her, amazed.

'I never knew you felt like this. You're always so efficient, and everything you do goes well,' she said.

'Well, I've grown a carapace now,' said Frances. 'And I've acquired a status of my own because I've made a go of the shop. But I've learned that if I want to have any sort of social life, a successful career isn't enough of a passport on its own; I must be twice as bright and twice as gay as if I'd a husband under whose protective flag I could sail out into society. I must be ready for wolves who think I'll be an easy lay because I must be missing it—and they may be among the ranks of my so-called happily married friends—and I must never be woebegone or demanding. I need friends, I'm not going to wrap the rest of my life around Clive and make him into a mother's lambkin, so I've learned my lesson. And now that I've settled for Geoffrey, things are a lot easier all round. Officially I'm manless still, but in fact I'm not.'

Sarah had listened to this outburst in astonishment.

'I suppose your children are still so young, and tie you so much, that you haven't thought things out this way yourself,' Frances went on. 'But it's common experience. It must be much the same for Paula. I know she's got Eric, but just look at him. *Faute de mieux*, wouldn't you say?'

'You might marry Geoffrey,' Sarah said, her head reeling. 'Don't you hope to?' She snatched at one concrete part of Frances's thesis to expand.

'No. He'll never leave his wife, and if he did I wouldn't want him round me all the time,' said Frances. 'Not now. I've been on my own too long, and thank God I don't just need a meal-ticket; I supply my own But I'm glad to have him in the background, I admit.'

'Someone else might turn up.'

'Someone married, maybe. But where will you find a single man old enough for me—or even for you. You must have discovered they simply don't exist.'

'No bachelors?'

'If they're still bachelors in their forties, they're either too gay, or queer, or too inhibited,' Frances declared.

'Divorced men, then?'

'All the divorced men I've ever come across have had their next wife lined up before they've got their decree,' Frances said.

'I don't know any widowers,' Sarah mused. 'There's old Mr. Briggs, he's a retired gas inspector, in Shenbury, He's eighty-four. But there are lots of widows around.'

'Female longevity,' said Frances brusquely.

'Do you want to get married again?' Sarah asked.

'No, I don't. At first I couldn't contemplate anyone after Tom. Then, when I began to think a bit differently, I discovered how limited was opportunity. Now I'm glad to be on my own. But I'd miss Geoffrey, if he took off,' she admitted. 'I curse him sometimes, but I'm glad of him. What about you, though? What about Michael?' Frances knew that Sarah had seen him a number of times since the party.

'Oh, it's finished.' Sarah turned away. The shop was empty. It was early-closing day in Culverton, and there was seldom much doing in the last half-hour before one o'clock.

'Oh, what a pity. What happened?'

Paula had not asked this question. She had simply accepted the disappearance of Michael in the same incurious manner in which she had registered his entrance into Sarah's life.

'I was a simpleton, I suppose,' Sarah said. It was suddenly a relief to talk about it. 'I was naive enough to think that he might, eventually, want to marry me. He seemed to like the children, and they liked him. It turned out just as you said. He only wanted an affair.'

She picked up a copper bracelet from among a collection laid out on a piece of blue velvet and inspected it. 'I suppose he's one of those gay bachelors you were talking about.'

Frances thought it perfectly possible that Michael had a wife already, somewhere.

'Wouldn't an affair have been a good idea?' she asked. 'He's quite attractive, and good company.'

'Oh, Frances, how could I have an affair? With the kids and all? It would have been asking for even more problems than I've already got. It's different for you, Clive's older, and away from home. And you had a decent marriage, presumably. I didn't, and I want one, but I can see I'm not going to get it.' Sarah groped in her battered handbag for a handkerchief and blew her nose hard. 'Sorry for the outburst, but you asked for it. I'm just a bit depressed today. I don't see how I'm to go on managing. I need to marry someone with some money, who can pay for us,' she said.

'Well, I see what you mean,' said Frances. Poor Sarah; things were too much for her today, but she'd brace up again. Frances knew about resilience. 'I'm sorry about Michael.'

'A clandestine intrigue's no good to me,' said Sarah. 'I want a bit more than that.'

'You'll get another chance,' Frances said. 'You're young enough. Limbo needn't last for ever. Here's your mother coming.'

3

As one o'clock struck, *The Spinning Wheel* was closed,
and Mrs. Getteridge, Frances and Sarah walked down
the street to *The Bell*. A table had been booked, as the
hotel was always busy in the middle of the day. The two
younger woman admired Mrs. Getteridge's hair-do;
Madeleine had blued her hair and set it in smooth
waves; she looked quite chic in her lavender suit, her
plump and remarkably unlined face slightly flushed
after its toasting session under the drier. They went
straight to the dining-room; Mrs. Getteridge did not like
bars. However, once they were seated at their table,
she ordered sherry for them all while they read the
menu.

Their table was by the window. Mrs. Getteridge sat
with her back to it, while Frances and Sarah sat at
either side of her.

'What will you have, girls?' Mrs. Getteridge asked,
delving into her bag for her spectacles. 'Turbot sounds
nice. What about that?'

'I'd rather have roast lamb, please,' said Frances.

'I'll have the turbot,' said Sarah, hoping to please
her mother by accepting her suggestion.

They gave their order, and sat back sipping sherry
while they waited for their asparagus soup.

'I invited Edith to join us, but it's her bridge day,'
said Phyllis.

'Do you play, Mrs. Getteridge?' asked Frances.

'No. I haven't time for such things, I have a lot to do
at home,' said Phyllis.

'Yes, I'm sure you have. Being a doctor's wife must be interesting,' Frances said. She thought Sarah's mother a foolish, complacent woman, and it would have been amusing to have led her into an exposition of her own vacuity, but that would only hit at Sarah indirectly. Instead, Frances set out to charm. She asked for and received a full description of the telephone answering device which released Mrs. Getteridge from her post quite often, and another of the garden and the house. Sarah relaxed, leaving the conversation gratefully to Frances. How very nice other women were, she thought, with warmth; one's girl-friends could be depended on to close ranks and help in times of stress; they needed no lengthy explanations; intuition was enough.

The meal ground on. The turbot was rather insipid, but the lamb was good.

'When Jan and Felix are a little older, I hope Sarah will come and help me in the shop,' Frances said to Mrs. Getteridge.

Sarah woke up. She had been dreaming while she ate her gooseberry tart.

'What?' she said.

'Your mother was wondering how I could manage the shop on my own,' Frances said. 'I've just been telling her that I need some help, and I'm hoping you'll give me a hand two or three times a week.'

Sarah gaped. This was news. Frances had always seemed to her monomaniacal about the shop.

'Felix will be off to the grammar school soon. In any case, he could have his lunch at school, like today, couldn't he?' Frances plunged on. During the meal she had made up her mind to take Geoffrey's advice. She did need help in the shop; he was right. If she had more time, she could investigate other lines they might stock, and in time expand; there was room for it in Culverton. And Sarah urgently needed some escape from her solitary life in Shenbury. There might be fewer Marston pots for sale, but financially she would break even if she could enlarge her scope.

'What will you do if Felix fails his entrance?' asked Mrs. Getteridge, totally ignoring the implications of Sarah's proposed career.

Sarah brought her attention to bear upon the question. She had been picturing herself racing round her chores at home and catching the bus to Culverton with Jan.

'He'll go to the secondary mod., of course,' she said.

'I should have thought his father would want him at a good school,' said Mrs. Getteridge querulously.

'Culverton Grammar is excellent,' Frances said. 'I often wish Clive was there.' This was not strictly true, but she had a great desire to oppose this vapid woman.

'Martin begrudges every penny he sends us,' Sarah said. 'He'll never stump up school fees. Anyway, he's off to South Africa soon, and I don't suppose we'll get anything after that.'

There, it was out; her mother had heard the worst.

'Just explain, please, Sarah,' Mrs. Getteridge said.

Sarah did so, while her mother spooned up strawberry ice-cream. Only time would show what Martin meant to do, she said; and even if he were ordered to continue payments, it would be extremely difficult to enforce them after he had left the country.

'You'll want that job, then, won't you, Sarah?' Frances asked.

'It looks as though I'm going to need it,' Sarah said.

4

Mrs. Getteridge made a business of settling the bill and calculating the tip, implying that she was rarely placed in the position of having to undertake this task. Sarah was accustomed to her mother's maladroit management of such things, and was not embarrassed, but Frances thought the affair a calculated act, since no grown woman could in fact be so green; she grew angry over the affectation, which effectively destroyed the original generosity of the invitation.

They trailed from the dining-room in single file, among the tables which were placed very close together in order to admit the maximum number of diners at any one time. Mrs. Getteridge led the way, and Sarah came last. At a table near the door, plodding through the pallid turbot, David Watson was sitting with another man. Sarah had noticed him earlier; his back was towards her, and he had not seen her. Now she wondered whether to speak to him; he seemed engrossed in talk with his companion. However, the matter was settled, for Mrs. Getteridge, in passing down the narrow aisle between the tables, dealt the other man a hearty blow on the head with her handbag. In the resulting confusion of apology, David, rising to speak to Sarah, pushed his own chair back against that of the person behind him. There was by now some fair degree of chaos in this corner of the dining-room, and two waitresses began to hover anxiously.

Sarah introduced her mother. David already knew Frances slightly, since he sometimes went into *The*

Spinning Wheel for parcels that Anne had ordered and left to be collected. His wounded friend accepted Mrs. Getteridge's apologies with good grace, and made haste to condemn the overcrowding in the room.

'Will you bring your mother round for a drink to-morrow evening?' David suggested to Sarah, having discovered that Mrs. Getteridge would be in Shenbury for two more days.

Sarah had an impulse to ask if Anne would mind, and pulled herself up sternly; surely David was allowed occasionally to use his own initiative. She accepted, but Frances, who was also asked, had to refuse; Geoffrey was coming the following day.

'What a charming man,' exclaimed Mrs. Getteridge as they walked away from *The Bell*. 'So nice-looking, with that grey hair.'

Sarah was surprised by this glowing reaction to David; he rarely seemed to figure as a person in his own right, usually appearing as the husband of Anne, or the father of Joanna and Malcolm; but he must have another life here in Culverton, as a business man with an identity of his own. It was true that his dark hair had turned very grey lately, and a man in his forties without a trace of baldness automatically acquired an aesthetic advantage over his less well thatched brothers.

'Yes, David's very nice,' Sarah agreed. 'But rather indecisive.'

'You're getting very intolerant, dear,' Mrs. Getteridge said. 'You mustn't find fault so much.'

Sarah and Frances exchanged a glance at this blatant pot-calling.

'Have you time to come in for coffee before the bus?' Frances asked, knowing full well that they had not.

'I'm afraid not,' Sarah said. 'But thanks.'

'Well, goodbye then. Thank you for the lunch, Mrs. Getteridge,' said Frances, grinding out the words.

'Delighted, my dear,' said Mrs. Getteridge. 'I know how good you are to my poor girl.'

Her poor girl made a most unfilial grimace behind her mother's back.

'Come on, Mother. We must get a move on,' she said, and shepherded her mother off down the steet. Culverton was quiet now, with only a few cars parked at the sides of the normally busy thoroughfare. It was a fine afternoon, though a fresh breeze made it cool. Scattered groups of people strolled along, gazing in the windows of the closed shops. Sarah and Mrs Getteridge window-shopped their way to the bus stop.

'Shall you be able to manage working for Frances, dear?' Mrs. Getteridge asked, when they were seated in the front of the bus, bowling along the leafy lanes where tall chestnut trees, laden with their blossom candles, were ranged on either side.

Sarah had been wondering this very same thing, always supposing that Frances's offer had been serious; it must have been, for she would never propose something of this nature lightly. Mrs. Getteridge's words, however, had the effect of making Sarah immediately wave aside the obvious difficulties as of no account.

'Oh, I'll find a way to fix things,' she said airily. 'There won't be any problem.'

Mrs. Getteridge said no more, merely pursing her lips into a disapproving line. Jan and Felix were destined to become latch-key children, it seemed clear; delinquency would follow, but it was not for her to interfere. She settled herself more comfortably in her seat and looked out of the window. At least the scenery could be admired without provoking controversy.

'How fresh the trees are looking,' she remarked. 'What a pretty time of year.'

5

Felix went to tea with Jackie Phipps at the garage the next day, much to his grandmother's disapproval. Sarah had to telephone for him to be sent home before she and her mother went up to the Manor, since she would not leave Jan alone. Mrs. Getteridge did not care for Felix's choice of friends, especially when he came back covered in oil, having spent a happy time in Mr. Phipps' inspection pit. She left Sarah to clean him up and help Jan put Algernon and Claud back into their hutches after the airing they had been allowed in a wire enclosure on the lawn, and walked back to Meadow Cottage to change for the evening's engagement. She was righteously fatigued, for she had helped Sarah during the day to wash chaircovers, curtains, and clean out cupboards, and not before time.

Sarah settled the children down with their homework. They promised to give themselves supper and go to bed if she was not back by eight. Then she went upstairs and changed into her pink linen-type dress; Paula had got it for her through an offer from *Home Fair*, cut out and ready to sew, and it was at least new and a cheerful colour. She put on her matching lipstick with a lavish hand, blued her lids and blacked her lashes, and walked off up the village, feeling gay.

At Meadow Cottage she waited in the garden until her mother and Edith, who had also been invited, should appear. Peonies and lupins flourished in Edith's border, anchusa cascaded in great blue waves, and the air was full of summer scents.

'How elegant we are,' Edith said, as they all set off together. 'We must hold our own, you know, Phyllis, with Anne, who's sure to be in a snappy little number from Hartnell. Come along, we'll be late.'

They went in her car, Sarah with her long legs crammed into the back. It was not very far, but Phyllis at least was pleased to be spared the walk after her rigorous day, and Sarah gained a sense of occasion from riding in such style, all dressed up. It was her first evening out since the end of her affair, if anything so slight could be called by such a name, with Michael.

Mrs. Getteridge had always been extremely gratified that Anne Watson acknowledged Sarah socially; to have one's errant daughter *persona grata* at the Manor compensated for some of her failings; she had met Anne once, on a previous visit, and now looked forward to renewing the acquaintance and displaying the fact that Sarah had a very respectable family in the background.

When they drew up on the gravel sweep in front of the Manor, there, unmistakably, was parked Dennis Baker's motor-cycle. Sarah was surprised to see it, for she did not think that Dennis figured on Anne's visiting-list, but perhaps he had been invited in order to be asked to perform a service, such as running the tombola at the village fête; or perhaps, since David had started the rot with his invitation the day before, Anne had decided to make it a plebeian occasion all round. Everything became clear, however, when David appeared at the front door, which stood hospitably open, to let them in.

He led them through the hall and into the drawing-room. French windows opened on to the lawn, and the evening sun slanted through them, filling the big room with golden light. There, standing by the fireplace, glass in hand, stood Dennis. No one else was present.

'Anne's away for a few days,' David said. 'She'll be sorry to miss you, Mrs. Getteridge. Now, what can I offer you?'

Very soon a remarkably gay party was in progress. David poured out generous drinks for everyone, and they all sat round in Anne's deep-sprung, gold brocade-covered chairs, talking. Edith questioned Dennis about his doings at the school; she liked him, and was sorry for him, recognising his kind heart and hopeless plight as he gazed across the room at Sarah. But he responded to her interest, and grew talkative, and felt that he was quite a social success at last.

Sarah, free of the feeling of inferiority which Anne Watson always generated in her, also shed her defensive approach to her mother's presence.

'I hope that wasn't an important client Mother nearly laid out yesterday, David,' she said.

'Oh, so do I, Mr. Watson. I am sorry. It was clumsy of me,' Mrs. Getteridge twittered. 'The room was very crowded.'

'It was the managing director of Fanshawe's Paper-mills,' David said. 'We're doing a deal about some wrappings. He didn't mind, he wants our order. In fact I asked him and his wife to come this evening, but they were already going somewhere. He was very disappointed.'

'I'm glad we didn't wreck negotiations,' Sarah said.

'Not at all. His opinion of me rose when he discovered I knew you,' said David, grinning. He looked directly at her as he spoke, and Sarah thought, good heavens, David's flirting with me! What would Anne say? Well, and why shouldn't he, poor chap! He didn't get much fun.

'Where is your wife, Mr. Watson?' Mrs. Getteridge asked, for all the world as if she had read her daughter's mind.

'Oh, in London, visiting her parents and buying clothes,' said David. 'Her family love having reunions on the slightest provocation. Our Spanish couple is away too, as it happens.'

Strange coincidence, Sarah thought. Anne wasn't going to be left doing the cooking if she could help it.

'So you're all on your own? Oh dear!' said Mrs. Getteridge, thinking with complacence of the excellent arrangements she had made for the welfare of her husband before she came away, the pies and cakes left ready, and the instructions minutely written down for faithful Mrs. Bragg to carry out each day.

'To tell you the truth, I'm thoroughly enjoying it,' said David, and it was clear that he was. He showed them round the garden, explaining his plans for even more improvements, showing off his asparagus beds and floribunda roses. They visited the ponies in the field, and admired the water-garden. Coming past the outbuildings on their way back to the house, Dennis asked what the various sheds were used for, and David showed them where his garden tools were kept, bright and gleaming, neatly ranged in rows, and then his workshop. He was making a cupboard; even to an uninformed eye it was a skilled and expert piece of work, waiting to be assembled on his bench. Dennis asked David if he did much carpentery, and when they returned to the house David, with diffidence, showed them a stool he had made, and a small table; it was crafts-man's work.

'I never knew you did this, David,' Edith said, examining the beaded edging on the table, which was in David's study. 'How did you come to take it up?'

'When I was at school we had a very good chap who taught us how to use tools,' said David. 'Later on I mended bits and pieces here, and then I taught myself the rest. I enjoy it.' He looked a little sheepish, thus caught out in his enthusiasm.

'I knew you painted,' Edith said. Her eyes strayed to an easel, folded up against the wall, and some canvases stacked against it, with only the backs visible. David did not offer to display his paintings.

'Well, I wanted to be an architect when I was young,' David said. 'I didn't finish my training, but I like to keep my hand in. I draw and sketch a bit. Now come along, your glasses must be empty.'

He shepherded them back into the drawing-room before they could uncover any more of his hidden talents; briefly, then, in the room that was so clearly imprinted by Anne's personality in its choice of furnishings, David faltered and lost his new-found confidence. But then he seemed suddenly to shrug off again his sombre mood; he poured more drinks, and began to talk to Dennis about the Test Match.

At length Sarah said they must go. The delicate French clock that stood on the mantelpiece said ten minutes past eight.

'Are you on your own for supper, David?' Edith asked. She exchanged a glance with Sarah, who had invited her back, with Mrs. Getteridge, to Spring Cottage for a cold meal.

'Oh, I'm quite a cook. I shan't starve, Edith,' David assured her. He banged his knee with his hand. 'I wish I'd thought of asking you all to eat here. It's a pity to break the evening up so early. Why don't you stay? I'm sure there's plenty in the larder.'

'We've got to get back to the children, David,' Sarah said. 'Or at least, I have. I'm not sure quite how much there is at home, but we've masses of eggs at least. Wouldn't you and Dennis like to come back with us?'

Dennis's face lit up with simple joy.

'Well, what a splendid thought,' said David. 'But in that case I'll bring a contribution. I'm sure there's a tin of tongue, and some strawberries in the deep-freeze. Come along, Dennis, lend me a hand and we'll see what we can find.'

The two men disappeared, returning very soon with a large basket full of provisions, and clutching several bottles. Both wore happy grins.

'We'll go ahead, then,' Edith said, approvingly. Sarah would win over this; by the look of it, there would be plenty of broken pieces left over from the feeding of the five of them to keep her and the children going for several days.

In the end only sugar and salad dressing were required from the stores at Spring Cottage. David had produced lettuces and hock, as well as tongue. They ate with their plates balanced on their knees in Sarah's sitting-room, Edith and Phyllis reclining at their ease while the other three did the serving; David kept topping up everyone's glass, so that even Phyllis grew genial. She and Edith went away at last in the car, and David did the washing-up while Sarah and Dennis dried and put away.

122

'Now let's go and look at your pottery works, Sarah,' said David, when the last dish was done. 'You've seen all my working premises. I've never seen your wheel, you know.'

'Haven't you?'

Anne had many times been in the shed during production, and Joanna and Malcolm had used quantities of Sarah's clay.

'Never,' said David.

'Well, come on, then.'

It was dark now. Outside the back door the black bulk of the shed loomed up at them through the violet light.

'Don't fall over the strawberry nets,' Sarah warned.

'I'll lead the way,' said Dennis. He seized her hand, bold now that night surrounded him, and began to sing, idiotically, 'Don't fall over the strawberry net with anyone else but me,' as he set off down the path, towing her. David started to sing too. He caught hold of Sarah's other hand and they blundered down the garden, all ridiculously chanting the refrain, until, giggling weakly, they reached the shed.

'Heavens, we must all be thoroughly plastered,' Sarah said, letting go of her companions' hands to open the door. She switched on the light inside. 'Let's hope the kids haven't woken up, they'll think their mother's on the downward path even further than before.'

'Well, at least, for your reputation's sake, there are two of us with you here, not just one,' said Dennis, greatly daring. This was a dashing remark to come from him.

'Rather a pity, if you ask me,' David muttered, very low, so that only Sarah heard him. She snorted with laughter. Really, David was on form tonight.

'Here's the wheel,' she said. 'Have a go.'

So there in the shed, at eleven o'clock at night, they proceeded to make pots.

'You'll have to demonstrate,' said David, and watched while she took some wet clay from under a cloth in the bin, shaped it between her hands, and threw it on to the wheel. She made several pots, one after another, and David made a crooked saucer-shaped bowl. While this was going on, Dennis sat at the loom and wove some irregular rows of the tweed that was on it. Finally they decided to go back to the cottage to finish the wine, and Dennis led the way back along the garden path.

Sarah stopped at the door of the shed to switch out the light, and David stopped too. As she closed the door he took hold of her hand and kissed her lightly on the mouth in the concealing darkness. Then they followed Dennis, who was singing again, to the back door.

There was enough wine left in one of the bottles for one more glass each, and then Dennis, who had walked with David down to Spring Cottage carrying the food and the wine, remembered that he had left his motorcycle at the Manor.

So the two departed together up the road, arms linked, the most unlikely couple, both singing 'Don't go into the strawberry bed with anyone else but me.'

They're thoroughly, sloshed thought Sarah when they had gone. Let's hope no one looks out of a window and recognises David. Anne would scarcely be pleased at this prank if it were discovered.

And I think I'm rather sloshed too, Sarah decided, weaving her way back into the house.

She felt extremely dull and flat after they had gone.

6

The next morning David called at Spring Cottage on his way to work, carrying a large bundle of asparagus. He seemed none the worse for the evening's junketing.

'I thought you and your mother might enjoy this,' he said, handing the bundle to Sarah.

'Oh, how lovely! Thank you, David,' Sarah said. 'But you know, we've done very well out of you. There's stacks of that tongue left over.'

'Good. Then you needn't go down to the butcher.' said David.

It crossed Sarah's mind that it was Anne who had paid for the tongue David was being so free with, but this was no moment for pride. She took the asparagus from him; its fat green stems were cool in her hands.

'Well, thanks anyway,' she said. 'This will be delicious.'

'We had a great evening,' David said. 'I haven't enjoyed myself so much for ages. Where's Jan? Has she gone yet? I thought I could give her a lift.'

'She's upstairs cleaning her teeth,' said Sarah. 'The bus doesn't go till half-past. I'll call her.'

'There's no hurry. She won't be late. I'm early this morning,' David said.

He leaned against the garden fence looking as if he had hours to spare. Sarah, hearing his car stop in the lane, had walked down to the gate to meet him. Now she stood with the bundle of asparagus held against her pale blue shirt. Her arms, bare to the elbow, were very white.

'Did you get home all right without meeting P.C. Brown?' she asked. 'I thought you and Dennis might have spent the night in the cells.'

David laughed.

'No. We escaped undetected. No buckets of water on our heads either. I filled Dennis up with black coffee before I let him go. He must have got home safely or he'd have sent for me to bail him out.'

'No thick head today? I'm not hung over, and I must say I deserve to be,' said Sarah.

'Oh, we weren't as far gone as all that,' said David. 'We could do with a few more evenings like it, here in Shenbury.'

'Oh, but you lead a very gay life, David,' Sarah said. Anne was always having dinner parties, when she had her Spaniards.

'It depends what you mean by gay,' said David, who never chose the guests. Before he could enlarge on this, Jan emerged from the house.

'Hullo, Mr. Watson,' she said.

'Hullo, Jan. Good morning. How are you on this fine May morning?'

'Oh, very well. It's tennis,' Jan informed him. She carried, he saw, besides her satchel, a somewhat battered tennis racket.

'Mr. Watson's giving you a lift,' said Sarah.

'Goody. That will be super,' Jan said. 'Goodbye, then, Mum.' She stood on her toes to receive Sarah's kiss, and then went hopping down the path ahead of David. For a crazy instant Sarah thought that David was going to kiss her too, as he had the night before.

'Lunatic woman, you must be still a bit high,' she told herself crossly, standing in the road and waving as they drove away. Still muttering to herself, she went back into the cottage where Felix was finishing his breakfast and feeding Dick with scraps of toast.

'What's that?' he asked, pointing at the asparagus. Sarah told him.

'It's a great delicacy,' she said.

'Hm. Looks like bluebells to me,' said Felix. 'There's a smashing film on in Culverton about motor-racing. D'you think Gran would take me if I asked?'

'I'm sure she wouldn't, and I forbid you to do any such thing,' said Sarah. 'You're a dreadful scrounger, Felix.'

'Well, if I clean Mrs. Fisher's car, she'll give me half-a-crown. Jackie and I could hitch in.'

'You'll do no hitching, my lad,' Sarah said. 'And you two boys certainly aren't going on your own. Maybe Jackie can get round Mrs. Phipps to take you on Saturday.'

'If she won't, I'll ask Dennis. He will,' Felix said comfortably. He got up and began hauling his blazer on over his plump arms.

'Mr. Baker to you,' said Sarah automatically. It was all too true. Dennis would do anything for anyone.

She put the asparagus on the draining-board; it was very young and fresh; there was scarcely any white showing at the ends, where still a little earth was clinging. At least this was David's own, to give away if he chose; he had grown it.

But Anne had probably paid the bill for the original crowns that started off the bed.

7

Mrs. Getteridge's visit came to an end at last. Edith lent Sarah her car to take her mother to the station; she had three ladies coming to Meadow Cottage to play bridge that afternoon, and did not need it returned at once, so Sarah seized the chance to do some heavy shopping. Then she called at *The Spinning Wheel*. The shop was full. The fine weather had brought the first tourists to the area, and many locals seemed to have called in with time to spare, if not money to spend. Sarah soon found herself helping Frances to serve the customers.

'It's true that you need help,' she said when at last there was a lull. 'I thought you were fabricating that, maybe, for mother's sake.'

'I'm never frivolous about business,' Frances reproved. 'I meant it. Have you thought about it?'

'Not in detail. You didn't say what you'd got in mind.'

'Well, mull it over in the next few days,' said Frances. 'I'll pay you thirty bob a day and your bus fare, and you could start with two days a week to see how it goes. Wednesdays and Fridays, they're the busiest. Then we can work up to more later on if it suits us both, and fix a weekly wage.'

'What about the holidays? I don't see how I could come then.'

'No, nor do I, at present. I'll get used to you and miss having some help. I think I could get a reliable sixth-former, though. They're always wanting holiday jobs, and I usually have one at Christmas, as you know.'

'Oh, what a good idea,' said Sarah, very relieved.

'Most of those senior girls at the High School are very dependable,' said Frances. 'It would work all right like that, I think.'

'You're on, then,' said Sarah promptly. 'But what if one of the children were ill?'

'I'd curse. But we'd have to weather it,' said Frances. 'They seem a healthy pair. If it doesn't work, I'll tell you frankly, Sarah, and no hurt feelings. This isn't a charity measure. I do need someone, and you're reliable, and it will do you good to get out of Shenbury for a few hours. It ought to suit us both, and so we'll both want to make it a success.'

'I'll start next Wednesday, then,' said Sarah. 'I'll come in on the bus with Jan.'

'You can go home with her too. You needn't stay late,' Frances said. Better to accept at the outset that some limitations were unavoidable.

So, the following Wednesday, Sarah started work at *The Spinning Wheel*. Before that day, she had an inch trimmed off her hair, and she made a navy blue rayon skirt from a remnant bought in the market. A sense of occasion fired her: she knew the shop so well already that there was nothing strange to dread; the day rushed past.

The next Saturday Paula came round to Spring Cottage for the evening. She had not been home the previous weekend, for Eric had persuaded her to go home with him to Aldeburgh to meet his mother, so they had plenty to talk about.

Sarah described the progress of her first week's work.

'I think it will be all right,' she said. 'I enjoyed it, there were people in and out all day. And Jan liked having me with her on the bus.'

'I'm sure she did. I don't see why it shouldn't be a

most satisfactory arrangement to you and Frances,' Paula said. 'She's a reasonable person, she'll understand if you do have to miss an occasional day because of the kids. After all, she knows what it's like; she's got Clive.'

'She doesn't seem to let him cramp her style, somehow,' said Sarah. 'I suppose he's just had to fit in.'

'Well, he's away most of the time,' Paula pointed out. 'And he always seems busy in the holidays, from what you say.'

'We won't grow rich on my earnings,' said Sarah. 'Still, I'll be able to put in more time if Frances wants me. She seems to be thinking of expanding, if she can get hold of the place next door.'

'She'll need you full-time if she does that. You'll have to get her to put you on a commission basis then,' said Paula. 'I expect she'll pay you more when you've got more experience.'

'She's pretty tight over money,' said Sarah, and then thought she was being most ungrateful, for who but Frances would have been content to employ her on such sympathetic terms?

'Well, she's had to learn the hard way herself,' said Paula. 'It can't be easy, keeping Clive at school.'

'How was Aldeburgh?' Sarah felt it was time to show some interest in Paula's doings.

'Grisly beyond belief. Eric's mother lives in one of those shingle cottages, you know, with a thatch coming down over the windows like a hat over someone's eyes, shutting out the light and letting creepy spiders and things into all the rooms. And she has four cats, and smothers all of them and Eric too with mother-love. It explains Eric, anyway. In fact I'm amazed he manages to be as independent as he does, now I know what goes on in the background.'

'Was she nice to you?'

'Scarcely seemed to notice me. I had terrible asthma most of the time, from the cats, or from nerves, or both,' said Paula. 'I'd forgotten how cats used to make me sneeze and pant. I don't often meet them these days, and four, with their hairs all over the place, is a lot to cope with.'

'It sounds as if you had a gruesome time,' said Sarah. 'Poor you. What will you do about Florence now?'

Eric wanted Paula to go with him to Florence in September. Paula said, cynically, that his wish for her company was simply so that he would be provided with transport thither in her car, and he knew that she would make all the arrangements. She was eager to go to Florence, but not anxious that Eric should be her comrade on the trip.

'Oh, I don't know. I'm not keen,' said Paula. 'Why don't we hire a caravan and take your kids to the sea instead? It would be much more fun.'

Sarah thought it would be tremendous.

'But it wouldn't be a rest for you. You'd go back to work with your nerves all a-jangle,' she said. 'And it would cost a fair bit.'

'It mightn't,' said Paula, who was willing to pay for it all but knew that Sarah would never accept. 'We could find out.'

'I'd thought of putting an ad. in *The Lady*, or something, to see if I could get a job cooking in someone's holiday house, where I could take the kids along,' said Sarah. 'If we just got our board and lodging it would be worth it.'

'No holiday for you,' said Paula.

'Well, I don't need one. It would be a change. Someone else's sink. Jan's looking rather washed out. She's

131

growing so fast. Some sea air would buck her up.'

'Well, no harm in trying, I suppose,' said Paula, who thought it sounded a frightful idea. Sarah would never have a minute to herself. Still, it was disheartening to have every plan you put forward shot down by your friends, so she made no further comment. Sarah might not find such a post, and in that case the caravan proposal might be resurrected. 'What are Anne and David doing this year?' she asked.

'I've no idea. Don't they always take a house at Frinton? I imagine they'll be doing that again.'

'I'd have thought Joanna and Malcolm were getting a bit big for sandcastles by now.'

'Oh, you can do other things there. There's tennis and golf,' said Sarah. 'Joanna told Jan.'

'Well, poor old David. It must be pretty dull for him,' said Paula. 'Still, he's so spineless I suppose he doesn't notice.'

'We had a terrific evening with him while Mother was here,' said Sarah. 'Anne was away. Did Edith tell you about it? David was quite different. You know how he hardly opens his mouth while Anne's around? Well, he never stopped talking, and cracking jokes. He was quite a riot, in fact.'

'I'm delighted to hear it,' said Paula. 'He doesn't often slip his lead, poor wretch. I'm surprised he dared. I thought Anne had thoroughly emasculated him.'

'Hey, steady on!' protested Sarah.

'Well, all he ever seems to do is fetch and carry. Even his business isn't his, but Anne's father's. But he must always have been very self-effacing or he wouldn't have knuckled under so meekly, unless he's just plain lazy.'

'He's not lazy. Look how he toils in the garden. And

all that carpentery. Did Edith tell you about it? His work is expert.'

'Well, everyone has to have something, I suppose. David must be basically a creative type; didn't he want to be an architect or something? He's probably a mass of snarled-up frustrations.'

'It must be pretty frustrating to be dependent on your wife for everything,' said Sarah.

'Yes, and if David was half a man he wouldn't wear it,' Paula said. 'I suppose he earns his pittance at the works. That ought to make him master in his own house.'

'It isn't his house, though. And he probably keeps quiet for the sake of peace. One does.'

'I wonder if Anne enjoys her power?' Paula mused. 'A cleverer woman would contrive things so that it seemed to be David who footed the bills. The blatant way she talks about paying the school fees and the builders and what-not makes me blush.'

'I expect it's all piled up so gradually they didn't realise what was happening,' Sarah suggested. 'After all, Anne is a kind person; she can't have wanted to hurt David. Look at what she's done for me and the children.'

'Only because it suits her,' Paula said.

'You're very hard on her.'

'She gets away with trampling on people because she's loaded with money,' Paula said. 'But maybe she's lost her sensitivity because of David being so spineless. Who can tell which happened first?'

'Like Frances getting tough since she was widowed? She can't have been before. Circumstances change people, of course,' Sarah agreed. 'Look at me.'

'Oh yes, tough as they come,' teased Paula. 'You're

as vulnerable as Jan, and you know it.'

'Well, I soon won't be,' Sarah said. 'Wait till I've been a business woman a bit longer. I'll be hard as nails.'

'Even Mother's tough,' Paula said. 'One has to be in life, or else go under, it seems to me, especially if one's alone.'

'Mother's tough, but in a different way. It's all connected with being married so satisfactorily. And Caroline. They lean on their husbands and wear a sort of "I'm-happily-married-so-no-one-can-hurt-me" kind of armour, and nothing else seems to matter very much.'

'It makes them rather dull, don't you think, with respect to your mum?'

'Yes I do,' Sarah admitted. 'They're cloying, with their sancity-of-marriage act. But maybe I feel like that just because I'm jealous. I don't know. I really prefer the company of my fellow limbo ladies like you and Edith and Frances, to that of the happy band of matrons.'

'Limbo ladies? What a gorgeous expression!' Paula burst into delighted laughter. 'It's often quite a pleasant sort of limbo, isn't it? Like now?'

'Yes, I admit that this is very agreeable,' said Sarah sedately. 'Still, male company is nice too, in its proper place. Do you think there are any limbo men?'

'If there are, Eric's one,' said Paula.

'And perhaps poor David is too. Dominated to destruction.'

'What did Frances's husband do?' asked Paula.

'He was in insurance. They lived somewhere in Surrey and he commuted to London every day. Frances adored him, but she says she hated the one-upmanship among the wives—you know, my husband's car is bigger than yours, and my little girl is in a higher form, and so on. I don't think she's ever got over losing Tom.

134

She's just grown a protective skin over it, and she's prickly about being on her own, though being a widow is highly respectable, goodness knows.'

'I wonder why she came to Culverton? One would have expected her to go to London.'

'She likes the country, although she doesn't seem like a country person,' Sarah said. 'And she didn't think she'd like the rat-race in London. She likes being her own boss and she might have found it harder in London.'

'Well, the competition's keener, but I'd have thought there were wider opportunities,' Paula said. 'Since I've obviously got to settle for being a career girl for the rest of my days I think I'll look for a more interesting job. Listen to me, complaining about my lot, when half our mail at *Home Fair* is from frustrated wives longing to break out of their kitchens. No one is ever satisfied.'

'The Carolines of this world are,' said Sarah. 'And I must admit that I am, sometimes. When the sun's out, and the children are well, and no one's badgering me, and the garden is looking nice, and you're coming down for the weekend, then I'm content. But when I look ahead, into the future, then I panic.'

'I don't wonder.' Martin was sailing for Capetown in June, and with him went any sense of Sarah's financial security.

'Of course, I can always sell up here and find a job housekeeping for some desperate widower with five children,' said Sarah. 'You see such people advertising.'

'You'd go mad, after being your own boss,' said Paula. 'Or else you'd marry the widower and no longer be able to give your notice. I should stay as you are, if you can.'

'I reckon you're right,' Sarah agreed.

As she came to this conclusion, the telephone began to ring.

'Who can it be, at this hour?' It was nearly eleven o'clock.

'Dennis, I expect, to say "Goodnight, beloved," ' Paula suggested, and got a cushion flung at her as Sarah left the room to answer the summons.

Paula lit a cigarette. From the hall she could hear small, distressed, monosyllabic sounds. When Sarah came back, her face was quite white.

'What is it?' It could not be the children; they were safe upstairs, in bed. Something must have happened to Dr. or Mrs. Getteridge.

'That was father,' Sarah said. Then, seeing Paula's expression, 'He's all right. There's nothing wrong at home. It's Robin. Poor Robin.' She sat down and put her face in her hands. 'Poor Robin's dead.'

8

'But what happened? Was it a car smash? How frightful!' Frances said, when the next Wednesday Sarah told her about Robin. She had met him once, when the Muirs had paid a fleeting visit to Shenbury some time ago.

'He had a heart attack. He'd just mown the lawn. Caroline found him in the garden. He died in hospital the same evening,' Sarah said. She was still stunned by the news, still shocked with horror.

'God, how awful! What a terrible thing to happen,' said Frances. 'What will they do?'

'Goodness knows. I suppose he was insured,' Sarah said. 'Rob was always very sensible.'

But he'd neglected himself. He'd overworked, and grown heavy and unfit.

Frances was thinking of the long, wasting illness through which she had nursed Tom.

'Well, he can't have known much about it. Perhaps that's some comfort,' she said.

'It's so cruel, such a waste,' said Sarah. 'Your Tom, whom you loved, and now good, kind Robin. Two people who were really needed.'

'Well, duckie, that's how it goes,' Frances said. 'Trite but true. Whom the gods love, and all that. I'm so sorry, Sarah. He was special in your life, I know. Now brace up. It's nine o'clock. We must open shop.'

Since she heard the news, Sarah had been unable to think of anything else. She had telephoned, offering to rush up and be with Caroline, planning in her mind that she would ask Mrs. Phipps to have Felix, and Edith to have Jan, for a few days; but Caroline's mother had arrived, so she was not needed. She could not even go to Robin's funeral: 'strictly private', said the notice in the *Telegraph*. Her mind was haunted by memories of the past, of Robin as a young man, solemn and industrious; then by an image of him lying in the garden, helpless and forlorn, until found by Caroline. What a dreadful shock for her; what a terrible experience; all communication between them ended without warning.

Later, on that Wednesday morning, as if to pile on the torment, Michael Sherard came into *The Spinning Wheel*. It was the first time that Sarah had seen him since the night when she had clung to what remained of her honour, as she had ruefully called it when telling the tale to Frances. His hair had grown rather long, and now curled shaggily about his ears; he looked scruffier than she remembered. She was agreeably surprised to find how painless it was to see him again, and felt thankful that he had not succeeded in wearing her down, watching him dispassionately as he bought a French casserole from Frances.

'Hi, Sarah,' he greeted her, as though they had parted only the day before. 'How's things?'

'Splendid, thank you,' replied Sarah frostily.

'You don't mean to tell me Frances has press-ganged you into her employ?'

'There was no compulsion,' Sarah said.

'Well, I'm delighted to see you've escaped from that boring village of yours,' said Michael. 'But both you girls are wasted here, in this rural wilderness. Why don't you take yourselves off to London, where the talent is?'

'Why don't you?' asked Frances.

'Well, funny you should ask. I'm going to Spain, in fact,' said Michael. 'To do a film. Then I may go to Peru.'

'Lucky old you,' said Frances, without envy. 'I'm sure you'll have a famous time.'

'I shall, never fear. Well, goodbye, both,' he cried, and was gone.

'Well, did that hurt much?' Frances asked with interest.

'Not at all, I'm happy to say,' said Sarah. 'In fact I wondered why I'd found him so attractive. He seems so immature, somehow, with that way of talking.'

'He wouldn't like to hear that, I'm sure,' said Frances. 'He's probably living in the mood of his latest script. I expect he acts out all his fantasies.'

'Do you think so? All kinky?'

'Hm. Yes. You must have been his home-spun period,'

Frances said. 'Maybe he was writing a domestic serial when he met you, and needed warm human copy.'

'Thanks very much,' said Sarah drily. 'And to think I wasted sleepless nights over him.'

'Well, I'm sure it was due to lack of competition,' said Frances generously. 'I expect you can find charms in even your faithful Dennis that you'd overlook if you were surrounded by fascinating swains.'

'Very likely,' Sarah agreed. She valued his kind heart and his constancy.

On her working days, Sarah and Frances lunched together. They shut the shop for an hour, and during the morning one of them would slip out to buy something to eat. Meticulously they divided the cost of these meals, and in addition Sarah, whose garden was now in full productivity, brought lettuces and greens in, to make up for the gas, coffee and milk she consumed. She was sure that being punctilious like this was important to the success of their arrangements, and Frances respected her motives.

'I've applied for a holiday post by the sea,' Sarah told Frances, while they sat drinking Maxwell House after lunch on this day. 'I'd already written when I heard about Rob. I saw it in *The Lady*. It was a box number, so I don't know much about it, except that it's to cook and housekeep for a family in Cornwall. I expect masses of people will apply, but I might be lucky. It didn't say bring your own kids too, but it said the house was large. No harm in trying, I thought.'

'Well, I hope it comes off,' said Frances, who at once had visions of Sarah's children fighting with those of her employer, but was too tactful to say so.

'Of course, Caroline may need me. I must go to her if she does,' Sarah said. She had a little wistful vision

139

of herself and Caroline and all their children happily sharing a cottage by the sea for a month. 'What about you, Frances? Why don't you take Clive off somewhere? I could mind the shop when Jan and Felix are back at school. They always go back before Clive; you could go in September.'

'Well, it's a thought,' said Frances. 'I wouldn't go with Clive—he's off to Brittany, in any case, to speak French. I might go somewhere later. We'll think about it.'

Geoffrey had murmured something about an antique fair in Brussels, suggesting she should come, and really, why not? A week or so abroad would do her good, and it would be more pleasant with Geoffrey than on her own. Sarah could certainly manage the shop, unless some calamity befell her children, and that was a risk that must be taken.

'I'd love to be left in charge,' said Sarah. 'I'm getting quite ambitious.'

PART SEVEN

1

Anne Watson sat up in bed in a pale pink bed-jacket reading her mail. Her breakfast tray, bearing coffee and grapefruit and wafer-thin toast, was beside her, and the bed was strewn with opened letters. Quickly she slit each envelope, read the contents, then tossed them on to one of three heaps; the envelopes went on the floor. Beside her, the second twin bed lay undisturbed beneath its chintz counterpane. David had slept in the dressing-room for years.

He came in before leaving for the office. Anne had recently begun breakfasting in bed while the children were away at school, and the custom suited both of them. David read the paper peacefully while he ate his eggs and bacon; he devised the ritual of coming up-stairs, knocking on her door, and bidding her goodbye before departing every day, to maintain the polite fiction that communication existed between them

Today he found her leaning against her pillow hold-ing a sheet of Basildon Bond in her hand and laughing in what was for her a hearty manner.

'This beats all,' she said. 'Read it.'

David took the letter. In a large, well-formed hand the writer applied for the post of holiday-housekeeper vacant as advertised; she described herself as a good cook, adaptable, accustomed to children and able to furnish impeccable character references. She would require no wages, merely her keep and that of her two well-mannered children who could sleep on inflatable mattresses in her room if space was restricted. It was signed, firmly, *Sarah Marston*.

'Well,' said David. He could think of no comment. 'Are those all replies?' He indicated the other letters on the bed.

'Yes. Mostly hopeless. A few possible. One or two promising ones,' said Anne. 'But I must give the job to Sarah, of course. I hadn't reckoned on someone with their own children, but if she's so desperate for a holiday, she must come.'

'Do you think so?' David read the letter again. It was very neatly written. He imagined Sarah at the kitchen table, making a fair copy. 'Mightn't it be awkward?'

'I don't see why. The house is large enough, goodness knows, and the children all get on well. It might be a great advantage to have them, in fact. Jo and Malcolm are far less quarrelsome when Jan and Felix are with them. And we know Sarah's capable. She won't pinch the gin or be out courting every evening. There's no one else who sounds as good. Some of these are students.'

'Wouldn't that be better? You could ask a student to do more. Two students, perhaps.'

'They'd be inexperienced. Sarah's a glutton for work, you know that. Look what she gets through in that hovel of hers, and now she's in with Mrs. Delaney. Besides, she'll be so grateful, she'll do all that we want, and more.'

'I think it may be awkward.' David repeated stubbornly.

'Not at all. It will be doing her a good turn.'

David shrugged. Policy was never made by him, anyway.

'Well, it's up to you,' he said.

'That's settled then. It saves a lot of trouble,' said Anne. 'I'll accept what she says about the salary, but I'll give her a cheque as a present at the end. She can't refuse that, I'll tell her it's for the children.' Anne began to gather up the letters. 'What a pity I didn't think of suggesting it to her in the first place. It never crossed my mind.'

'It might have seemed very insulting,' David said. He fiddled with the edge of the counterpane on the bed that was meant to be his. 'I don't like the idea of her running round after us,' he said.

'She won't have to. The kids will all pitch in,' said Anne, who usually spent her whole holiday lying inert in the sun if the weather were fine enough, while others fetched and carried.

'Well, it's your decision,' David said. He felt impelled to emphasise this, so that any consequence could be traced back to Anne's responsibility for the situation, though what he anticipated he could not have said.

'I'll ring her now,' said Anne, stretching her hand out for the telephone beside her. She did not notice David duck his head, as though he meant to kiss her, as he sometimes ceremoniously did, before he left for work.

He went away.

Sarah was very embarrassed when she learned the reason for Anne's call.

'But how awful, Anne!' she exclaimed. 'Oh dear!'

'It's not awful at all. I'm thrilled to bits,' Anne said. 'How could you know it was my advertisement? Come up later on for coffee, and we'll talk about it.'

So, at eleven o'clock on the dot, Sarah reported. She

found Anne, dressed in cream linen slacks and a matching silk shirt, stretched out on a garden bed on the terrace. She looked very elegant; Sarah felt awkwardly large and coarse, in her jeans and cotton sweater.

'But aren't you taking the Spaniards? And I thought you always went to Frinton?' Sarah said, sitting down in a chair and tucking her long legs up as inconspicuously as she could.

'Question one, the Spaniards are leaving, and can't be persuaded to stay through August. I don't want to start new ones in until we're home again. Question two, I decided to try somewhere else for our holiday this year. There's a sailing boat that goes with this house. Some friends of mine will be close by, they put us on to it. The children will be able to run wild; they may enjoy it more.'

'I see.' Sarah stared at the garden. From where they sat she could see the lawn running down to the fields beyond. David's shrubs flourished on either side; huge bush roses starred with blossom made vivid patches against the varied greens; it was beautiful and peaceful.

'Well, do you want the job, now you know more? Will you come?' asked Anne, smiling.

Sarah took no time to decide.

'Yes, please. It would be wonderful, Anne. I was so afraid of landing up with some Scottish laird and lairdess who might be grand and terrifying, and think me vague and feckless.'

'Well, I know you're neither, and the children all get on together. Jo and Malcolm will be delighted. It will be a great success. It's a big house on the top of a cliff, with a sandy cove below, and it's just outside a village. I expect the shopping will be a bit of a bore, but we'll have both cars down there and we'll manage. It's useful that you drive. I'll leave all the housekeeping to you. How blissful to know that you can cope.'

Anne realised that Joanna and Malcolm would have to understand the agreement. Still, they knew the world contained others less fortunate than themselves; if they understood that this was a business arrangement they would not think it wrong for their mother to relax, as she had every intention of doing, while Sarah toiled.

'We'll work out the details later,' Anne said. 'You'll have to go by train, I'm afraid. There won't be room in the cars, with all the luggage and our bits and pieces.'

'I'm sure there won't,' said Sarah. 'There's only one thing,' she added, and explained about Caroline. 'But I think her mother's staying indefinitely. I'll find out tonight, and telephone you at once. Will that do?' She could not agree to help Anne, and then change her mind if Caroline needed her.

'Of course,' said Anne. 'Your poor friend. I'm very sorry.'

'Yes, it's awful. I don't suppose she really knows what she wants to do,' said Sarah.

'Perhaps you could go to her another time.'

'Yes.' Sarah rose to her feet. 'Well, I'll be off,' she said. 'Goodbye.'

Anne watched her go, sitting there in her expensive chair, pretty, competent, and generous behind her enamelled façade. And utterly ruthless.

2

Sarah was surprised to find how quickly she got used to thinking in terms of potatoes for seven, fourteen baked apples at a time, and two whole cakes disappearing for tea; and to freedom from care about cost. Anne's housekeeping budget seemed to have no limits, and Sarah's sense of values underwent a considerable shock.

She started a routine straight away, getting up at six-thirty every morning to get ahead with the work, because that was the only way she could be sure of having the afternoon free. It was no hardship, for Sarah had always found it easy to rise early, and now, with the summer air warm and clear and the dew on the grass, it was a delight to be up when everything was quiet; she slept well, full of sea air, for the first time for months, and no longer spent hours in bed reciting nursery rhymes or the names of flowers beginning with Antirrhinum and working through the alphabet down to Zinnia in an effort to calm her mind so that slumber would follow.

The house was a solid Edwardian construction, not lovely to look at, but comfortable, with large, lofty rooms and heavy Victorian furniture. Sarah's bedroom looked out over the woods that rose up behind the house; it was furnished with a huge mahogany wardrobe and chest of drawers, and a large brass bedstead with a mattress that sagged in the middle. Joanna and Jan slept next door, and Anne occupied the biggest bedroom, which had a view over the sea and its own washbasin. The two boys were together on the top floor, and David was up there too, in what must once have been servants' bedrooms. Fortunately Sarah's children were not interested enough to comment on these domestic arrangements, which might have struck others of their age as unusual. Sarah supposed that David was used to his banishment; maybe he snored. Because he slept in another room did not mean that he never slept with Anne at all, she reflected one morning, making Anne's bed with hospital corners.

It turned out that David was another early riser. On the first morning, Sarah was in the kitchen sorting out saucepans and counting enough potatoes to peel for lunch, while the kettle boiled for tea, when he appeared.

'Good morning, Sarah,' he greeted her. 'I didn't realise it was you down here. I thought it must be one of the children.'

'Oh dear, did I make a noise? I crept down,' said Sarah.

'It was the plumbing I heard,' said David. 'The pipes run past my head. Couldn't you sleep?'

'Oh, I slept like a log,' said Sarah. 'But I usually do get up fairly early, and it's best to get on with things while the children are out of the way, I find. I was going to make some tea. You'll have some, won't you? What about Anne? Shall I take her some? Do you think she'll have woken?'

'Not she. She'd sleep through an earthquake,' said David. 'And she wouldn't thank you for tea at this hour. You didn't wake me, Sarah. I was getting up anyway.'

'Oh, good. Well, I hope the children will keep quiet.

Jan and Felix will probably be down soon, they're longing to explore.'

There had only been time, the previous day, to shop for necessary supplies, allocate rooms, unpack, and have a quick bathe in the cove below the house. The children had gazed longingly at the point where the coastline vanished into the distance, but they had all been sent to bed as soon as they had had supper, for they had made a very early start to the journey, and everyone was tired.

'Joanna and Malcolm won't hurry to get up, I'm sure,' said David. 'It seems to be a point of honour with them to lie-in because of rebelling against getting up early at school, or something.' He pulled out a chair at the big deal-topped table, while Sarah got out thick blue and white striped cups and saucers, and poured milk into a jug. 'It's a glorious morning. I'm going for a walk,' he said.

'Yes, it's lovely,' said Sarah. She glanced out of the window. The grass was still damp with the light dew, and the trees cast long shadows across its green expanse. A few clouds wisped across the blue of the sky.

'We'll be able to take the boat out today,' said David. 'Sarah, I hope you aren't going to find all this cooking and cleaning too much.'

'Oh, I won't.' Sarah moved to the stove as the kettle began to boil. 'I've just got to get organised, then it'll be fine. I'm so grateful to you and Anne. We'd never have had a holiday in any other way. Don't worry about me, I'm as strong as a horse.'

'I doubt that,' said David. 'Anyway, I want you to enjoy it and not be rushed off your feet all day. I'll do all I can to help. Let me be the shopper. If you give me a list every morning, I'll get what you want.'

'But it's your holiday, David. You don't want to be bothered with that sort of thing, that's why I'm here. And anyway, what about your painting?' She had seen him take from his car a stack of small canvases and his painting equipment.

'That's a frowned-on activity, to be indulged in secretly,' he told her. 'It's my escape. I haven't got my workshop here.'

'Oh.' Sarah did not quite know what to say to this. 'Well, you'll want to spend as much time as you can with Anne and the children,' she insisted.

'Anne will be quite happy sitting in the sun, when there is any, or nattering to the Palmers down the road, and the children can have stacks of freedom here, don't you agree? As long as they stick together, and don't bathe unsupervised. They can't come to much harm.'

'Well, yes. I suppose they may fall down the cliffs, but that's a risk at any age,' said Sarah. 'Felix doesn't swim very well. He hasn't had much chance to practise.'

'We'll get him going this year,' said David. 'Do you like swimming, Sarah?'

'Yes, I love it,' Sarah said.

'Good. Well, that's settled, then. I'll organise the children to help you, they can take turns to wash up and come shopping, and they can make their own beds. It will do them all good. Anne won't notice as long as everything's done.'

Sarah did not know quite what to make of this remark, so she let it pass. It was very agreeable, for a change, to be told what to do.

'We'll do a lot of sailing, and a lot of swimming, and a lot of fishing,' David went on, drinking his tea. 'We'll take picnics in the *Kittiwake*. We'll have a good time.'

'I'm sure we will,' said Sarah.

'Well, I'll be off now and let you get on,' David said. He got up and rinsed his cup and saucer under the tap, leaving them to drain at the side of the sink. Then he went out of the house, and Sarah saw him walking with long, easy strides over the headland away from the village where a field of cut corn shone golden in the sunlight. He returned to the house at exactly nine o'clock, just as breakfast was ready.

After this, he came down every morning soon after she did. He was so quiet that she never heard him until he came into the kitchen. They always had tea together; then he would vanish, sometimes to paint, and sometimes just to go off on one of his lone, mysterious walks. Several times he was downstairs first, and had made the tea when she arrived. She began to look forward to these quiet meetings. They talked about trivial things, the plans for the day ahead, sometimes more seriously about the children. Felix's swimming was coming along well; he had managed, puffing greatly, a width of the small cove at its narrowest point. Jan, whose school had a pool, was trying to do the crawl. Malcolm felt the cold and never stayed in very long, but Joanna was a good swimmer and enjoyed it; it turned out that she was urging her mother to make a pool at the Manor. Sarah could not help reflecting how greatly Felix and Jan would benefit, inevitably, if this came about, but she had an idea it would mean a lot more work for David, for pools needed cleaning and painting, and had motors that needed maintenance, she thought. Perhaps he would not mind; he certainly seemed to enjoy swimming himself, and zoomed along at a great rate with his face buried in the sea. Martin was a good swimmer too; watching the flounderings of Hugh Palmer one day, Sarah decided it must be very humiliating for a man to be so poor a performer in the water, somehow unmasculine, even if the fault were not his own. She thought irrelevantly that Michael Sherard probably could not swim at all.

Jan and Felix usually appeared soon after eight. They laid the breakfast table, then went off to potter on the shore or go prawning if the tide were out far enough. At half-past eight Sarah felt that the noise of the Hoover was permissible, and she ran it quickly round the down-stairs rooms; it acted also as a summons to Joanna and Malcolm, who were as reluctant as their mother to leave their beds. But it was just as well that no one was anxious to swim before breakfast, she thought, hasten-ing around trying to get as much done as she could in this precious interval before the house was full of noise and movement.

The days ran into one another. As David had pro-phesied, Anne paid no heed to how things were done, as long as they were done; she often praised Sarah's cooking and told her friend Leila Palmer that they would all be putting on pounds whilst fed so well.

Leila was a hearty woman, not at all like Anne. She organised games of rounders on the sand after tea, with her own four children and every other child she could press-gang into joining the teams. Leila played herself, hitting mighty thwacks that sent the ball scudding to-wards the sea, and running briskly round increasing the score to loud applause from the spectators. Anne some-times acted as scorer, writing the runs on a child's slate held on her knee as she sat in a deck chair in what was likely to be a safe spot near the pitch.

David usually vanished before the game began. He and Hugh Palmer sometimes went down to the village pub, but more often David went off on his own, for Hugh seldom escaped the rounders game. Sarah played if ordered to by Leila, but she was usually busy in the kitchen then, preparing supper.

One day, fielding near Anne's seat, Sarah heard her talking to Leila, who was sitting beside her on the sand waiting for her turn to bat and yelling instructions to her team at intervals. Sarah was in rather a dream, not expecting the ball to come near her, gazing at the sea, which shone like glass for there was no breeze this evening, and hearing the sound of the little waves lapping on the beach as a background to the children's shrieks. The murmur of Anne and Leila's voices merged into this general symphony of sound; gradually Sarah realised that they were talking about David.

'He's much better tempered this year,' Anne was saying. 'Having that boat was a good idea. It gives him something to do.'

Guiltily, as if she had overheard something far more serious, Sarah moved away out of earshot. She had never seen David angry; he seemed infinitely patient, but given to long silences when he clearly had nothing to say. In the evenings, after the children had gone to bed, Sarah had developed the habit of clearing away the coffee things and then going up to bed herself, so as to leave Anne and David tactfully alone; she was sure they could not always want her with them, however politely they might urge her to remain. She had found a horde of paperback thrillers in a cupboard in the house, and was steadily reading them, warm in her bed at night. She wondered sometimes what Anne and David talked about; she supposed they did talk, though there was no sound of voices in the house. Quite often they went down to the Palmers, or to the houses of other friends they had made in the village; several times they dined with some of these people at a hotel famous for its lobsters. She supposed they were enjoying themselves. This, after all, was their family holiday. Anne went to Davos every February.

The *Kittiwake* was a success, it was true, and David obviously enjoyed sailing her. Sarah often went for trips with him and his crew. She had done some sailing in the fateful summer when she met Martin, though never since then, but she had more experience than the junior mariners and was in demand as bo'sun for this reason. She was always willing to pack up a picnic meal for a trip to some distant rocky islet if the weather were fine. Anne seldom came on these expeditions; she preferred to go down to the Palmers and drink gin with Leila or play bridge if they could find a four, but she always urged Sarah to go, saying David could never manage all the children alone. Quite often there were Palmer children in the boat too; Hugh Palmer seemed to have no enthusiasm for sailing, and as he was such an indifferent swimmer this was doubtless just as well; Sarah could not make him out, he seemed quite a kindly man, and she knew he made a lot of money in advertising, but he presented a very negative front to the world, she thought. Leila, of course, had enough drive for both of them.

When told such things as that he would not be able to control the children and the boat without Sarah's aid, David was never stung into making a sharp retort, and Sarah marvelled at his restraint; sometimes she wished he would, it seemed so sheepish just to suffer it; but after a time she decided that he was so used to overt criticism that he scarcely noticed it any more. She often longed to stick up for him, since he would not do it for himself, and had to remind herself that she was only the help.

Sarah, in her bedroom in the evenings, wrote about all this to Paula. She praised Anne lavishly as an employer, for no one could have been more generous or less interfering, but she described also Anne's habit of handing out ten-pound notes to David for the shopping in much the manner that she might give the children ice-cream money. 'He's very quiet when she's around, like he is at home,' wrote Sarah. 'But he's quite different when she isn't there.'

This was true. In the *Kittiwake* he was transformed, an authoritative skipper who brooked no argument from his crew, and knew just what he was doing. He seemed to grow in stature in the boat; then, when they got back to the house, he shrank again into insignificance. In fact he was quite a tall man, nearly six foot, but he was slight, and did not give any impression of size or of physical strength; he was strong, though; all his gardening must have built his muscles up, Sarah thought, watching him hoist the sails of the *Kittiwake*, boom and all, on to his shoulder as if they were no heavier than a garden rake.

In the boat, Joanna and Malcolm were at peace with one another. Sarah began to notice that they only quarrelled when their mother was in earshot and might be appealed to for arbitration. They enjoyed lighting camp fires in sheltered nooks on rocks to fry sausages, and obeyed any instruction from David or from Sarah instantly. If David gave them a command in the presence of Anne they usually moaned, until she said, 'Do as your father says,' when they grudgingly gave in.

Sarah became more sensitive on David's account after one evening when the Palmers arrived for drinks. For once Leila had deserted the rounders game, which was in noisy progress in the cove below; she had given her knee a twist the day before and feared to aggravate the injury. They sat round in deck chairs while David poured out drinks, and they idly talked about their children, their children's growth, and their children's forthcoming exams: all children nowadays had forthcoming exams, no matter what their age and circumstances. Sarah had noticed that they seemed to have few other things to talk about; world politics, or art, or books or music, for instance, seemed not to interest them at all. She left when the Palmers arrived, and disappeared into the kitchen, but David was sent by Anne to bring her back.

'You don't have to include me all the time, really David,' she protested.

'Anne sent me, but I'd already started on my own account,' said David. 'I need some support, Sarah. Please come.'

At this, she gave up arguing, and went with him back to the garden, where she sat meekly beside Hugh, holding her glass. Hugh was lamenting because his sons' school had just put up its fees; what with that, and the university to follow, not to mention the two girls, where would it end?

'I know, it's awful,' Anne agreed. 'I've just paid a huge bill for Joanna's new uniform, she's grown out of every stitch; and Malcolm needs a dinner jacket. Then Joanna says she must have a new pony, Freddy's too small for her now.'

A dinner jacket, Sarah thought. Malcolm in a dinner jacket, aged twelve. Whatever next?

But Anne was going on.

'And I've just paid the builders over a hundred pounds

for a few minor repairs in the house,' she said.

Sarah saw Hugh looking at David, who seemed quite unruffled.

'Let me fill your glass, Leila,' he was saying calmly. Sarah could not understand why he did not dash it to the ground in fury. She turned to Hugh and asked him frantically if he had read *War and Peace*. It seemed an insane remark in the context, but it was all she could think of on the spur of the moment. He looked surprised, but replied civilly that he had never had the time. Sarah had read it during the long evenings of the years when she had been married and Martin had been off on his own pursuits. She had read a great deal in those days, though now all she ever seemed to read were thrillers. As they politely skirmished round this diversionary red herring, the rest of the company discovered that the last cigarette had been smoked.

Hugh, appealed to, forgot about Tolstoy with some relief, but had no cigarettes.

'Oh, David, that's too bad of you,' Anne was scolding. 'Can't you even see to the cigarette supply? You'd better go down to the pub and get some.'

'I'll go.' Cheeks aflame, Sarah had sprung to her feet.

'No, stay where you are, Sarah,' ordered Anne. 'David will go. There's some money in my bag on the hall table.'

David said nothing, but he did not go into the house. He walked round the side to where the Volvo was parked. Sarah heard him start the engine. She would not have been surprised if he drove off at top speed and never returned, but he went down the drive at his normal calm pace. After a short interval she made some excuse to the group on the lawn and withdrew to the kitchen. This time Anne let her go.

She saw David return. He parked the car in its usual place and walked past the kitchen window carrying two hundred filter tips, apparently undisturbed.

3

The summer weather varied, as it always does in England. There were several sequences of fine, sunny days, usually with a sharp breeze which sent the *Kittiwake* scudding along, the water creaming at her bow and her excited crew leaning well out to balance her as she heeled over with the wind. But between these stretches came intervals when it rained continuously, and the sea was grey, specked with the breaking crests of the rollers. Everyone grew fretty at these times. The children played Monopoly, or Racing Demon, or Canasta. The old, well-thumbed books that were in the house were pulled from the shelves and read. Brisk walks were taken to the village, where more up-to-date paperbacks could be bought. During the spells of bad weather Sarah racked her brains to think of diversions for the children. She got them playing all the paper games she could remember; she took them, wrapped in oilskins and wellington boots, for long walks; she had them making toffee in the kitchen. Fortunately Leila Palmer was as determined an organiser indoors as out; she embarked on charades and amateur dramatics for which a large cast was necessary on several occasions, and this helped; the Palmers, too, had a ping-pong table in their house. Each time the appeal of all these various alternatives to swimming and sailing was exhausted, the weather changed just in time, and the sun came out.

David became morose during the spells of wet. He seemed almost as sulky as the children, crouching in a chair in the sitting-room with some book or other that did not appear to interest him. Anne was the one who survived best, for she did not particularly care for the ploys that the rain prevented everyone else from enjoying, except for lying in the sun. She would meet Leila for coffee in the village, sometimes taking a child or two with her; she had her hair done, and went shopping for curios; she and Leila took all the children to visit a nearby stately home. Once she took the boys to Truro; they went to the cathedral, had a large lunch in a hotel, and spent the afternoon in the cinema.

This expedition was such a success that when the next period of bad weather came, Anne telephoned to Leila and they arranged a trip to Plymouth, taking all the children.

'Would you mind if I stayed behind?' Sarah asked, told of this arrangement. She had a mountain of ironing to do, accumulated because the rain had stopped the washing from drying. 'I could have a good clean-up all round, and do some baking,' she explained. It might also be less embarrassing for Hugh and Leila if she were not there, like a rather over-grown *au pair* girl, ever present. 'Jan and Felix can stay behind too.'

'Certainly not. They must come,' Anne said at once. 'But by all means you stay, Sarah, if you prefer. It will give you a chance to catch up, I see that.'

'I expect you'll be late back if you go to the cinema,' Sarah said. 'I'll have a good hot meal waiting.' The

thought of a day spent quite alone was suddenly alluring.

In the end, Hugh and David contracted out of the
Plymouth party too; they set off instead in Hugh's car
for Land's End, where neither had ever been. Briefly,
Felix and Malcolm toyed with the idea of going with
them on an all-male trip, but the flesh-pots of Plymouth
seemed more inviting on the whole; there would be
warships in the Sound; there would certainly be a cinema. They set off in the Volvo with Anne and the girls;
Leila and her passengers joined them on the road, and
they left in convoy.

By half-past nine everyone had gone and breakfast
was washed up. Sarah made herslf a cup of coffee and
sat down in the sitting-room to drink it, enjoying the
calm. There was only the sound of the rain on the windows, and the sigh of the wind outside. She forced herself into the kitchen at last, and set to work. She made
three cakes, some flan cases and jam tarts, and a huge
cottage pie for supper which would come to no harm
if kept waiting in the oven. Then she laid the table ready
for that meal. After that she went upstairs and gave
Anne's bedroom a thorough cleaning, so that it shone,
and smelt of furniture polish; to add the final touch, she
went out into the rain-soaked garden and cut a few sod-
den roses, which she shook vigorously and put in a vase
on Anne's dressing-table.

She had cold beef and salad for her lunch, deriving a
simple pleasure from carving it off the enormous cold
sirloin in the larder; until this August, she had never in
her life cooked such huge cuts of meat. After lunch she
resisted the urge to go to sleep in the armchair, and
started, instead, on the ironing. There were shirts for
everyone, jeans, and two of Anne's linen dresses which

she treated with special care. She hung all her finished work around the kitchen to air, and her mind was almost a total blank while she waded through the pile of washing.

She heard the back door open and close just as she had spread an old grey shirt of David's on the ironing board; it was frayed round the collar and cuffs, and a button hung loose; she must remember to mend it before putting it away. The sound of the door, when she expected to be alone, did not alarm her, for she knew at once who had entered the house.

He came into the kitchen, still in his raincoat, with his old tweed cap dripping in his hand. Sarah began to iron the shirt.

'You're back early. I thought you'd be the last one home,' she said. 'You can't have been to Land's End and back already.'

'We gave up. It seemed that every other holiday-maker in Cornwall had the same idea,' said David. 'The traffic was nose to tail all the way. And Hugh's got some sort of chill in his stomach, so we came home. I've left him drinking brandy and studying form in some racing paper.'

'Did you walk up? I didn't hear a car. You're simply soaked,' said Sarah.

'Yes. It seemed a shame to turn poor old Hugh out again just to bring me back,' David said. Anne's Porsche was sacred: no one else, not even David, ever drove it; at present it was snug in the garage. David had been dropped at the Palmers' by the party in the Volvo that morning.

'Have you had any lunch? How about some coffee?'

'I've had lunch. We stopped at a pub. And I've had quite a bit of Hugh's brandy, too,' said David. While they had been talking, he had taken off his raincoat and hung it over the back of a chair; it dripped on to the floor, forming a small puddle with remarkable speed. He laid his cap on the chair too.

'Have you had a nice peaceful time?' he asked.

'Yes, thank you,' Sarah said. She had finished the shirt now, and there was no more ironing, so she switched off the iron, coiled up the flex, and started to fold up the board. But while she was doing this, David started to walk towards her. It seemed like a slow-motion film to her, aware of his approach as she struggled to collapse the stiff old board.

'I'll do that,' David said. He took it from her, folded it efficiently, leaned it against the wall, and then caught hold of her gently by the shoulders. For a moment he looked at her, very intently, before he kissed her. Then he slid his arms round her body and kissed her again.

Sarah tried to resist. She stiffened her back and tried to keep her mouth closed, but she could not keep it up. Before she realised that her defence had gone, her arms were round David's shoulders and her hand was against the back of his head so that his mouth was tight against hers. She could hear the pounding of her own blood in her ears, and she could taste the sweetness of David's lips and his tongue.

While all this was going on, she told herself sternly that here was what Frances had described, the lonely husband looking for comfort, and if ever one needed it, this was he. Then she forgot about Frances and stopped thinking of anything except the present moment.

At last David said, 'I've been longing to do that ever since the night at your cottage.'

She remembered his gentle, chaste kiss in the darkness as they closed her work-shed, while Dennis pioneered the route back to the kitchen door. She had scarcely thought of that night again. Poor David, had it really meant something to him?

As he started to kiss her again, Sarah began, coldly, to calculate: Anne and the children would not be back for several hours, unless they too were defeated by the traffic. It was unlikely that Leila would allow her plans to be thwarted by mere tourists; they would surely go on with the goal of the cinema ahead; a very good film was known to be showing. David went on kissing her while she worked this out, and very soon, even if she had wanted to stop him, the power to do it had left her; her bones seemed to melt into jelly as they clung together, hanging on each other's mouths.

Sarah had always supposed that adultery must of necessity be sordid; now she found otherwise. She shed all sense of guilt as she discovered a tenderness to which she could respond in a way she had not known was possible. She found that David, in spite of his ardour, needed encouragement, and she was glad to be no timid virgin whom he must lead.

Afterwards, they lay in her strange, creaking, brass-steaded bed, and she stroked his thick, grey hair, and ran her hand gently down his cheek and over the sparse, dark hairs on his chest, while she thought, when we go home I must put this completely out of my mind, as if it had never happened, but I'm very glad that it has.

'What a funny bed this is, Sarah,' David said, bouncing to make it squeak. 'Do you dream, lying here all alone?'

'Not much,' said Sarah. 'I usually go straight to sleep.'

'You won't now, darling,' David told her. 'You'll think of me, every night. Won't you?'

'Maybe,' Sarah said. 'Till we go home.'

'I'll be thinking of you, too. I lie upstairs in my attic thinking about you, darling Sarah. I love you.'

'Do you?' She wondered if it were true, or if he felt he must say so, to stop her from feeling too wicked and sinful. But she did not feel wicked or sinful.

She felt wonderful.

'Darling David,' she said, and felt a great wave of tenderness for him engulf her as they turned to each other again.

PART EIGHT

1

'We must think about Christmas,' said Frances. 'It will soon be here, and we must order anything extra we want, or it won't arrive till the New Year.'

It was the beginning of October, and she had just returned from Belgium, fizzing even more than usual with energy. During her absence Sarah had looked after the shop, and everything had worked smoothly; she had enjoyed her strenuous week.

'We're almost out of Marston pottery,' said Sarah now. 'I think we could handle quite a consignment of it.'

'Sure. Bring in as much as you like,' said Frances expansively. 'It goes very well at this time of the year.' She consulted her stock list. 'We'll sell a lot of costume jewellery, too; I did order quite a batch just before I went away. Sarah, you found you managed all right, did you, coming in every day?'

'Oh yes. It was great, I thoroughly enjoyed it,' Sarah said.

'Hm. Well, I'm wondering about that lease next door. I think it might be very stupid of me to pass up the chance of getting it, but I'd need you full time. It would mean quite a financial outlay for me, but I think we'd get it back in no time; there's room for much more quality stuff in the town and I'd like to see us handling stationery and perhaps paperback books, maybe even some second-hand stuff—jewellery I mean. And we could carry much more than we've room for here, we could stock a bigger range of our present lines. I'm going to talk to the bank manager about ways and means. Geoffrey thinks I should do it.'

'Well, I'd be delighted to come in every day,' said Sarah. 'The only trouble would be the holidays, but it might be possible to arrange something, I suppose. I might let you down, though, if there was a crisis.'

'Well, that's something that can happen in any circumstances,' Frances said. 'People have old mothers and so forth. Don't let's worry about it too much yet. I realise you wouldn't want to let the children run wild in their holidays, but if you could do just a bit then, I could probably manage with a student for most of the time. I mean to play this rather cool, or the price may go up.'

The shop next door was at present a tobacconist's dark lair; if *The Spinning Wheel* were to be enlarged, much painting and opening up of the place would be required. Sarah thought it would be rather exciting if they undertook this; it would be challenging to come in to work every day and still keep things running at home; with Martin in South Africa, too, she would have to solve in some fashion the problem of how to manage about the children in their holidays, since she would be compelled to become a full-time earner.

'How's Paula?' Frances asked her now. 'She finally went, did she?'

'Yes, I had a card from her last week.'

'When does she start her new job?'

'Not till the New Year.'

Paula had burnt her boats and decided to leave *Home*

Fair. She had found a position with a firm of hardback publishers who had a thriving homecraft list where she was to be an editor. At present she was in Italy with Eric; they had been to Florence and were now in Rome. Sarah had scarcely seen her since her own return from Cornwall.

'Well, I hope her holiday will be as successful as yours was,' Frances said. 'It was rather a gamble, wasn't it?'

'In what way?' Sarah, who was polishing glasses, turned her head away so that her expression could not be seen by the observant Frances.

'You might all have got on one another's nerves, and spoiled your life in Shenbury. The kids could have murdered each other, or David could have made a pass at you. Perhaps he did?'

'What, with four children around all the while? Such things need opportunity, surely?' said Sarah, with superb nonchalance.

'Well, no one could blame David, that's certain; he seems to have a dim time of it, from what I can make out,' said Frances. She hesitated, and then went on. 'Sarah, while I was away I heard something about the Watsons.' She tapped her pencil against her teeth. 'It wasn't just malicious gossip, the person really knew what had happened. I wonder if I should tell you?'

'Well, having got so far, I think you must,' Sarah said, with great calm. 'Is it some juicy scandal?' she asked, trying to keep her voice light, but her mouth was suddenly dry.

'You could say so. It's about a hectic affair Anne had, years ago. You hadn't heard about it, had you?'

'No! It can't be true!'

'It is. There's no doubt about it,' Frances said.

167.

At this moment the shop door opened and two women came in. Frances had to break off, and Sarah was forced to control her impatient curiosity until they closed the shop for lunch, for a steady trickle of customers filled the place for the rest of the morning.

'Now tell me about Anne Watson,' Sarah said at length, taking their re-heated Cornish pasties out of the oven. For some reason she felt unable to utter David's name.

'Well, I suppose you may as well know. Since I heard about it, you might just as easily some other way. But it was very well hushed up. I imagine not a soul around here has the least idea about it.' She watched Sarah tip the pasties on to two plates and add lettuce and beetroot. 'We must have chicory one day,' she said.

'Yes, we will. Don't digress, Frances,' said Sarah.

'Well, here goes.' Frances sat down and began to eat. Between mouthfuls she related what she had heard.

'I met this woman in Brussels,' she said. 'She was married to some tycoon out there, something to do with one of the big petrol companies I think. When she discovered that I lived in Culverton, she said. "That's where Anne and David Watson live, isn't it?" So I said, nearby. Remember, Sarah, I don't know them well like you do, I just know them from their visits to the shop, so I wasn't particularly excited about this link. But anyway, Geoffrey and I met this woman and her husband after dinner one night, and had drinks, and so she told me the story really for something to talk about while the men were nattering. It seems that years ago, just after they were married, Anne had a tremendous affair with some man in the Army, who was married. His wife discovered, and threatened to divorce him, and there was a fearful fuss about it because as long ago as that, the Army was pretty stuffy about such things as divorce, though it tolerated a certain amount of goings-on. For all I know it's still the same. Well, the man didn't want his career wrecked, so he chucked Anne and swore to be good. Anne's father pitched in, bought David into this business down here, bought the Manor and set them up. Hardly anyone knew about it. But this woman who told me was a friend of the wife of Anne's boy-friend. She had it straight from the horse's mouth, as you might say.'

Sarah had sat rigid, listening to this recital, forgetting to eat her pasty.

'I can't believe it!' she exclaimed. 'Anne, of all people. She's always so correct.'

'Well, I gather there were ways in which David didn't quite come up to scratch,' said Frances drily. 'It fits in with what you've told me about his craven demeanour at home.'

'I'm not sure if I understand you,' said Sarah.

Frances spelled it out for her.

'Well, my dear, if David's a poor performer, no wonder Anne strayed,' she said.

'But there's nothing wrong with David,' Sarah said, and then added hastily, 'There can't be. Besides, there are the children.'

'It seems there's some doubt about Joanna, anyway,' Frances said.

'Oh no! You must be wrong!' But Joanna bore no resemblance at all to David; daughters were supposed to take after their fathers, and Jan certainly had Martin's dark colouring and a look of him about the mouth. There was no rapport, either, between David and Joanna.

169

'Well, I don't suppose anyone will ever be sure. Anne, perhaps,' said Frances.

'But it's terrible! Why didn't David leave her?'

'He was bought, wasn't he? It was worth his while to stay. If he's impotent, or nearly, I don't suppose he really minded all that much,' said Frances.

Sarah could not answer.

'I'm not surprised that you're dumbfounded,' said Frances. 'Anne's probably had other affairs since then, but I expect she's learned to be a bit more discreet.'

Sarah's thoughts at once flew to Anne's frequent trips to London, when she was supposed to be visiting her relations. But how could David accept such a life? When all this began, he was young; he could have left Anne, and gone back to his training. Sarah remembered the sketches he had shown her that evening in Cornwall while they waited for Anne and the children to return from Plymouth; the plans of houses he would never build; the wispy, curiously indeterminate landscapes he had painted; the attempts at sketches of herself, delicately drawn yet indefinite; only the house plans were confidently done. Both of them were too exhausted with emotion that evening to talk very much, both trying to get back to normal before they were confronted by the rest of the party. David had gone for a walk later, so that he was out, down on the shore, when the Volvo returned from a successful outing.

After that, the holiday had continued as if nothing had happened. David and Sarah were rarely alone together, except in their early morning encounters, though they were often with the children while Anne amused herself elsewhere. Sarah felt that she and David were together on one side of a barrier that divided them from the rest of his family, but he gave no sign of feeling the same way; it was as if nothing had taken place at all. After a while Sarah began to wonder if she had dreamt their whole encounter.

But it had happened. And at the time it was wonderful. A chance had arisen, and they had seized it; that was all. It meant nothing, in spite of David's protestations in the excitement of the moment. There would never be a sequel, so the whole thing was best forgotten, Sarah told herself. But in spite of this brain-washing attempt, every morning when they met before the house was stirring, she hoped that he would kiss her, or at least say something to show that he remembered their delight together. But he never did. Sometimes, she thought he watched her when he himself was unobserved, but Anne could have been with them all the time and never found cause for complaint.

Since the return to Shenbury she had only seen David in the distance, in the car, or far down the garden working away; but she had seen plenty of Anne, whom she had helped to prepare the children's clothes for school, for the new Spaniards were not yet of any great value and it seemed second nature now to Sarah to lend a hand. Anne had given her a cheque for thirty pounds at the end of the holiday. The paper had seemed to sizzle in Sarah's hand, but she accepted it; she put it into Savings Certificates for Jan and Felix.

'Maybe David has affairs too,' Sarah said at last.

'Maybe. Maybe it's just with Anne that he can't function,' Frances said.

Sarah remembered David's diffidence; Frances had a point. For the rest of the day the subject was churning around in her mind. Surely David, when young, must have been as badly hurt by Anne as she had been by Martin? But if Frances was right, then Anne might have some sort of excuse for what had happened, and David's acceptance of the situation, however lamentable, was at least explained. Sarah was not greatly given to psychological delving, and she felt quite exhausted with the effort of trying to fathom the whys and wherefores of all this. She was very silent, sitting with Jan in the bus going home that afternoon, and when Dennis, faithful still, appeared in the evening hoping to be given supper, he found her very inattentive.

2

October, as so often, was a lovely month that year. The trees slowly turned yellow; the leaves began to fall; the michaelmas daisies, red, blue and purple, stood tall in the gardens, and Sarah cut great bowls of them to put in the cottage.

Paula lent her the car one weekend, and she made a lightning visit to see Caroline, whom she found withdrawn in her new isolation, and determined to go on living in the house where she had been so happy with Rob. Sarah felt it was very melancholy; the two boys were back at school, and Caroline and Fiona seemed lost, a forlorn pair in the big house all on their own. The garden was already getting out of hand, although Caroline had found some old man to help her with it. Sarah urged her to contemplate moving into something smaller, that she could manage more easily on her own, but Caroline seemed unable to think of anything practical;

172

Sarah supposed that she was still stunned and numb from the shock of losing Robin, and had not really faced, yet, what the future offered and would demand. She parried all Sarah's suggestions that she and Fiona should come to Shenbury for a visit; all she wanted to do was to be left alone.

Home again, Sarah settled down to make dozens of pots for the Christmas market. She painted them vividly, to cheer herself up with the gay colours, and invented several new designs. She sat at her wheel, trundling away, and wished continually that David would come to see her, but he never did. Faithful Dennis called almost every day, but David did not come.

She thought of him a great deal, moving about in the great house so near; she thought of his strange life with Anne, and his equivocal relationship with the children; and she remembered every moment of their love-making. If he had really meant what he said, why did he not come to see her? Surely it would not cause gossip in the village if he were to drop in once during six weeks, she thought, fiercely jabbing her thumb into the wet clay to hollow out a vase. Round and round went the growing vase; she drew it up between her fingers and lifted out the rim to make a lipped edge. Of course, he had not really meant a word of it. He was a despicably weak man who chose to live with a rich wife in conditions of utter humiliation, because he had not the guts to stand alone; likewise, he had snatched an illicit hour with her merely because the occasion offered. Maybe he had a regular mistress tucked away; Sarah could not believe that Frances's theories were correct. Perhaps his diffident demeanour was merely the line he played with women, masking the fact that he was a thorough philanderer. Round and round went the potter's wheel, and round and round went Sarah's thoughts, reaching no very great conclusion. The only certain fact was that David, in accepting his life as it was, had wasted years when he should have been developing as an individual; he was squandering his talents and his potential. Sarah fumed away, driving at her wheel, first castigating Anne for so emasculating David, then mentally berating him for letting it happen.

The stove flickered and went out. Sarah had forgotten to fill it that morning. It was a chilly afternoon, and she still had time for two hours' work before the children were due back from school. Cursing, she got off her stool, brushing past Dick who lay on the floor nearby, and rinsed her hands at the sink. Then she slouched crossly up the garden to fetch the paraffin from the coal-shed, where it was kept. She had just finished relighting the stove and was putting the cap back on the tin when she heard someone calling her outside.

It was the postman with the second delivery; he had a parcel for Jan, whose birthday it was in two days' time. It was from Caroline, who was her godmother. Sarah exchanged some badinage with the postman, who was quite a wit, and then went into the cottage to hide the parcel until the proper day. Seeing Caroline's writing on the label made Sarah think about her; she did a bit of lamenting over her, then paused in the sitting-room to talk to Dick, who had followed her back from the shed. At last she decided she could no longer postpone her return to work, and she went back down the path to the shed.

The door stood ajar; she sniffed, then opened it quickly, horror-struck at what she saw. Her loom, the wicker chair, and a cupboard where she kept paints, were all ablaze.

She did not wait to wonder what had happened. Forcing her limbs into action, she rushed to the sink and filled the pail she kept for mixing clay with water, and flung it on the fire. It hissed and sizzled, but the flames leapt on and caught at the legs of the wheel. Sarah filled the pail again and again, her eyes streaming from the smoke and the legs of her jeans singed by the fire, until she realised that she was losing the race. Then she tore back up the garden and into the cottage to dial the emergency service. The exchange answered at once, but giving her message seemed to take for ever. At last it was done and she raced back to the shed. It did not occur to her to shout or run up the road to find someone to help her. By this time smoke was billowing out of the shed, but she managed to struggle on with her buckets of water until the fire brigade arrived.

They put out the fire very quickly, so that she almost felt ashamed at calling them, but when they had gone only the bare shell of her shed was left. Her loom, the wheel, and all her finished work, were quite destroyed.

3

Dennis arrived. Quite a crowd, in fact, was present while the firemen worked; Shenbury rarely had such an excitement. However, the village policeman soon sent everyone away who did not seem disposed to be helpful. Dennis heard what had happened down at the school, and he came home with Felix, very fearful;

great was his relief at discovering Sarah apparently un-
hurt, though she was filthy from her struggles with the
fire; her face and arms were streaked with grime. Dennis stood with her dismally in the wreckage, and did his
best to console her and Felix; Jan, when she got back,
burst at once into tears, so that it was altogether a very
sombre group gathered in Spring Cottage that evening.
Dennis had to leave at eight o'clock as he had a meeting
at the school which he could not avoid; he promised
to come back the next evening to see how things were,
and to clean up the shed as soon as it had dried out
enough.

When she had eventually got the children into bed,
Sarah returned to the scene of the disaster. Since the
light was, of course, no longer working, she had to go
back to the kitchen for a candle, which she stuck in
a bottle and placed on the top of the charred remains
of the wheel. There was a sour smell everywhere; little
wisps of steam still rose from spots where the heat had
been strongest; everything was saturated with water.
Nothing at all was left of her possessions. She knew it
might have been very much worse; the cottage might
have caught; she might have lost everything; someone
might have been hurt. But it was bad enough. Now,
belatedly, shock set in. She started to tremble, and stood
huddled there in the near-darkness, her arms clasped
over her chest, shaking with the suppressed sobs of
acute nervous reaction.

David could not see her at first. The candle spluttered
on its perch, sending flickers of light across the black
interior of the shed, and he could hear the choking
sounds she made.

'Sarah, Sarah, where are you?' he called.

She heard him, and she recognised his voice, but she

could not answer. However, he made out her dark shadow crouched in a corner of the shed and crossed to her in an instant. As he bent down to her, she unfolded her long legs and was drawn up into his arms in a single movement. His hands touched her shoulders and smoothed her hair in frenzied little caresses, and he blindly kissed her cheeks, her forehead, her eyelids, and any part of her that met his frantic, searching lips. She smelt of smoke, and her face was wet, and he tasted the salt of her tears.

'Are you all right? Sarah, darling, are you all right?' he kept asking her, and she clung to him, sobbing afresh, with great shuddering breaths shaking her body. He wrapped his arms tightly around her and held her closely against him until her trembling gradually grew less. She began to move in his arms, mumbling something about needing a handkerchief, so that he loosened his grasp of her a little and fished in his pocket for his own. As he gave it to her, he felt her icy hand.

'You're frozen, Sarah. However long have you been out here? It's cold tonight. Come along into the house,' he said.

He led her back to the cottage while she snuffled into his handkerchief and dabbed at her face, all the time clinging to him with her free hand.

It was cold in the cottage, too, for she had gone out leaving the door open. David shut it, took her into her own sitting-room, drew the curtains and switched on the electric fire. She stood shivering in the middle of the room while he did all this.

'Darling, have you got any brandy? Or some whisky?' David asked, taking hold of her by her arms as he had that afternoon in Cornwall.

177

'I don't know. There might be a drop in the kitchen cupboard.'

'You go over by the fire while I look,' he said.

She heard him clattering about in the kitchen while she knelt on the floor in front of the bright orange glow of the fire. A little warmth began to penetrate her chilled condition. David soon returned with the remains of a small bottle of brandy tipped into a tumbler, relic of Paula's bounty.

'Drink it up,' he said, and held her against him while she sipped it. After a time she steadied down. David held her very firmly, as if he never intended to release her, with her hand that was not occupied holding the brandy glass imprisoned inside his jacket against his chest.

'You're not hurt, are you?' he asked her again, when at last she had stopped shaking.

'No, I'm perfectly all right. I don't know why I'm in such a state. Sorry,' she said.

'Oh, darling, what were you up to, setting fire to the place?' he asked.

'It was Dick. At least, it must have been. The postman came before I'd put the cap back properly on the paraffin, and Dick must have knocked it over, and it caught alight from the stove. Where is he, anyway?'

'Never mind about Dick. He's probably asleep on Felix's bed,' said David. 'It's you I'm concerned with. Finish this up. Do you feel warmer now?'

She nodded, and drank the rest of the brandy. David took the glass from her and set it down. Then he moved her gently from the floor to the sofa. He looked at her searchingly, an expression of great tenderness on his face. There was a smudge on her forehead; her hair was tangled; and she looked about fifteen years old. The brisk, efficient Sarah had vanished.

'I saw the fire engine on its way back to Culverton, but I didn't discover it had been here until after dinner,' he said. 'I came down at once. Sarah, I was so frightened.'

'Does she know you're here? Anne, I mean?' Sarah made an enormous effort to pull herself back into a composed, sensible state.

'Never mind about Anne,' said David, in exactly the same tone that he had used when speaking of Dick.

'Oh, but David—' Sarah began.

He started to kiss her again, and now that he was convinced she was physically unharmed by the fire, his concern changed and turned into urgency.

Into her neck, he said, 'I've wanted to come down here every day since we've been back from Cornwall. But what was the use? The only possible thing to do seemed to be to keep away, where I couldn't touch you.'

She thought, wearily, here we go again. He's had a fright, because he does care for me after a fashion, but not enough to risk his own security. At the moment I'm winning because of the accident. Tomorrow Anne will be top girl again. In fact, maybe she's not at home tonight, so he hasn't had to say where he is.

She was very tired, and it took her time to become aroused, but for weeks now she had longed for such a moment. Briefly the thought of the children crossed her mind, but because it was David who was here with her, the chance that they might be discovered seemed strangely unimportant.

4

He came round again the next evening. Although he he had promised to do so, Sarah half expected him not to turn up, but she had got rid of Dennis on the plea of needing an early night. She had washed her hair, and put on a dress; she felt tense and anxious, certain that she was in for more grief and disappointment.

'What have you said to Anne?' she demanded, breaking away from him after they had clung together in a long kiss. Already his touch was familiar to her.

'Nothing. I just slipped out,' David said.

Sarah thought, why struggle? I don't mind a scandal with David. I'm not ashamed. I'm not married, and the children would survive. He's the one to worry. He must set the pace.

She said, 'As I've lost my working equipment, I've decided to go into *The Spinning Wheel* with Frances. I'll get some money from the insurance company, and I'm going to put in the rest of Aunt Hilda's legacy. I'd thought about it before. Now I see I must do it.'

'Good God, Sarah, you're tough,' David said. 'You were practically fried alive yesterday, and now you've got your future all lined up.'

'It's no good drifting,' Sarah said firmly. 'I've done that long enough.'

'You're quite right.' David said. 'Have you fixed it up with Frances already?'

'No. But I know she'll take me in as a partner,' Sarah said.

David caught her up again in his arms, and sought her mouth.

'You're so strong, Sarah. You make me strong too. I'm different when you're there,' he told her.

She thought, I'm not, really. I don't want to be strong all the time. But I am stronger than you. Was this how it all began with Anne? You were weak, and she was stronger, and you needed her? And now you're weaker still, and she's quite domineering.

As he went on kissing her, Sarah thought then of herself. With the exception of dull, faithful Dennis, all the men who had ever been attracted to her had, in time, moved on elsewhere; here was one who, if he could produce some basic guts, might prove constant.

'Sarah, if I were free, would you marry me?'

She stayed very still in his arms.

'Well, you're not, so why talk about it?' she said, calmly.

'I could leave Anne.'

'If you did, then we might discuss it,' she said, and moved away from him. She could not think clearly when his hands were on her body and his lips were on hers. She crossed the room and watched him as he gazed at her beseechingly. She saw very distinctly that he needed to come to grips with some adversity; he should go off on his own, fend for himself in conditions of hardship and discomfort for a time, and so discover the strength of his own resources. But she feared that he lacked the spirit to leave Anne without first making sure of another haven.

'I wouldn't want to hurt her,' he said.

'Oh, David, hasn't she hurt you? She humiliates you twenty times a day,' said Sarah. She did not add, and she's teaching the children to despise you.

'She's generous.'

'It's easy to be generous with something you've got

plenty of,' said Sarah. But she must not be persuasive. This was something David had to work out for himself.

'I've loved you for ages, Sarah. Long before the holiday. You must have known how I felt. You're so—' he searched for the right word. 'So gallant, all the time.' He had come over to her again by now, and he caught her hands and began to kiss them. 'After that day in Cornwall, I didn't know how to keep away from you. I nearly stole down to your room lots of times.'

'But you never said a word. All those mornings, when we were alone, you never said a single word,' she reproached him.

'But you knew I loved you. I told you so,' he said.

'I thought you'd got over it the next day,' Sarah said, rather brusquely.

'I didn't see how we could hope for any future,' David said, lamely.

'And do you now?'

He was at the crossroads. Here was his chance to produce the nerve to bring his house of cards down round his ears, and put some meaning into his life before it was too late. He might never get another opportunity, and if he did not seize this one, he would lose his soul for ever.

'Anne might refuse to divorce me.'

'Well, then, when the new law is made you can divorce her, in five years' time,' said Sarah calmly.

'But then we couldn't get married for ages. Would you live with me? Openly?'

'I'd prefer to be married, of course,' Sarah said. Wild schemes rushed through her head. She could go in with Frances for a period, while David found his feet and turned himself into a man, and they could meet from time to time.

'You don't love me,' David said.

She thought, I don't know whether I love you, or whether I just need you. But you need me. Without me, you're lost.

'David,' she said aloud. 'I've only a certain amount of strength, and I've used a lot of it up already in my life. I don't think we could have made love together so wonderfully, as we have, if I didn't love you. But I must protect myself. What's the good of letting myself get involved with you if I'm never going to see you? I'm only going to get hurt again.'

He said, very calmly, 'I will leave Anne. I've planned it often. First I'll have to wind things up at the office, but that won't take long. I'm not indispensable down there. Then I'll go. I may find it rather hard, at my age, to get another job, but I'll find one in the end. When I've done that, if Anne will divorce me, will you marry me?'

'Yes, David,' Sarah said at once. She thought about his children fleetingly; he had never once mentioned them in this discussion. Was Frances right? Were either of them his, in fact? They were withdrawn, difficult children; perhaps they had been adversely affected by the non-communication between their parents. Jan and Felix were no problem; they were fond of David, and they could only benefit by having him around. She saw that she might relax her tough, independent attitude a little; the walls of Spring Cottage began to retreat as the prospects for her grew brighter; the world was suddenly larger.

'We couldn't stay here,' she said.

'Anne might go. Her father might buy her back again,' said David.

'I'll have to talk to Frances.'

183

'Yes.'

'If Anne went, there's the other shop. There might be a flat above it,' Sarah said. There was David's carpentry too; he might, at last, be able to earn his living by his own creative skill, but he would have to find this out for himself. 'We couldn't stay in Shenbury, that's certain,' she added, realising with a pang that Spring Cottage would have to go.

'Everyone will be outraged,' David warned. 'We're the sinners, don't forget.'

'Are we really? I wonder,' Sarah said.